Phoebe Cary, Alice Cary, Mary Clemmer

The Last Poems of Alice and Phoebe Cary

Phoebe Cary, Alice Cary, Mary Clemmer

The Last Poems of Alice and Phoebe Cary

ISBN/EAN: 9783337408442

Printed in Europe, USA, Canada, Australia, Japan

Cover: Foto ©Andreas Hilbeck / pixelio.de

More available books at **www.hansebooks.com**

THE LAST POEMS

OF

ALICE AND PHŒBE CARY.

EDITED BY

MARY CLEMMER AMES.

NEW YORK:

PUBLISHED BY HURD AND HOUGHTON.

Cambridge: The Riverside Press.

1874.

CONTENTS.

LAST POEMS OF ALICE CARY.

BALLADS.

POEMS OF THOUGHT.

CONTENTS.

LOVE POEMS.

POEMS OF NATURE AND HOME.

CONTENTS.

POEMS OF LOSS.

LAST POEMS OF PHŒBE CARY.

BALLADS.

    The Homestead.
    The Gardener's Home.
    The Mill.
    Sugar making.
    The Playmates.
    The School.
    Youth and Maiden.
    The Country Graveyard.

CONTENTS.

LAST POEMS OF ALICE CARY.

BALLADS.

——◆——

AT REHEARSAL.

O Cousin Kit MacDonald,
   I've been all the day among
The places and the faces
   That we knew when we were young;

And, like a hope that shineth down
   The shadow of its fears,
I found this bit of color on
   The groundwork of the years.

So with words I tried to paint it,
   All so merry and so bright —
And here, my Kit MacDonald,
   Is the picture, light on light.

It was night — the cows were stabled,
   And the sheep were in their fold,
And our garret had a double roof—
   Pearl all across the gold.

The winds were gay as dancers —
   We could hear them waltz and whirl
Above the roof of yellow pine,
   And the other roof of pearl.

We had gathered sticks from the snow-drift,
    And now that the fire was lit,
We made a ring about the hearth
    And watched for you, dear Kit.

We planned our pleasant pastimes,
    But never a game begun —
For Cousin Kit was the leader
    Of all the frolic and fun.

With moss and with bark, for his sake,
    The fire we strove to mend —
For the fore-stick, blazing at middle,
    Was frosty at either end ;

But after all of the blowing
    Till our cheeks were puffed and red,
No warm glow lighted the umber
    Of the rafters overhead ;

And after all of the mending,
    We could not choose but see
That the little low, square window
    Was as dark as dark could be.

The chill crept in from our fingers
    Till our hearts grew fairly numb —
Oh, what if he shouldn't see the light,
    And what if he shouldn't come !

Then pale-cheeked little Annie,
    With a hand behind her ear
Slipt out of the ring and listened
    To learn if his step were near ;

And Philip followed, striding
    Through the garret to and fro —
To show us how our Cousin Kit
    Was marching through the snow;

While Rose stood all a-tiptoe,
    With face to the window pressed,
To spy him, haply, over the hill,
    And tell the news to the rest.

And at last there was shout and laughter,
    And the watching all was done —
For Kit came limping and whimpering,
    And the playing was begun.

" A poor old man, good neighbors,
    Who has nearly lost his sight,
Has come," he said, " to eat your bread,
    And lodge by your fire to-night.

" I have no wife nor children,
    And the night is bitter cold;
And you see (he showed the snow on his hair)—
    You see I am very old ! "

" We have seen your face too often,
    Old Mr. Kit," we said;
" How comes it that you're houseless —
    And why are you starved for bread ?

" Because you were thriftless and lazy,
    And would not plow nor sow;
And because you drank at the tavern —
    Ah ! that is why, you know !

" We don't give beggars lodging,
    And we want our fire and bread ;
And so good-day, and go your way,
    Old Mr. Kit," we said.

Then showing his ragged jacket,
    He said that his money was spent —
And said he was old, and the night was cold,
    And with body doubly bent

He reached his empty hat to us,
    And then he wiped his eye,
And said he hadn't a friend in the world
    That would give him room to die.

" But it wasn't for you," we answered,
    " That our hearth to-night was lit,"
And so we turned him out o' the house —
    O Kit, my Cousin Kit !

As I sit here painting over
    The night, and the fire, and the snow,
And all your boyish make-believe
    In that garret rude and low,

My heart is broken within me,
    For my love must needs allow
That you were at the rehearsal then
    Of the part you are playing now.

THE FISHERMAN'S WIFE.

PEACE! for my brain is on the rack!
Peace of your idle prattling, John!
Ere peep o' daylight he was gone:
And my thoughts they run as wild and black
As the clouds in the sky, from fear to fear.
Mother o' mercy! would he were here —
Oh! would that he only were safely here —
Would that I knew he would ever come back!
Yet surely he will come anon;
Let's see — the clock is almost on
The stroke o' ten.   Even ere it strike,
His hand will be at the latch belike.
Set up his chair in the corner, John,
Add a fresh log, and stir the coals:
We can afford it, I reckon, yet.
The night is chilly and wild and wet,
And all the fishers' wives, poor souls,
Must watch and wait!   There are otherwhere
Burdens heavy as mine to bear,
Though not so bitter.   It was my fret
And worry that sent him to his boat.
Here, Johnny, come kneel down by me,
And pray the best man keep afloat
That ever trusted his life at sea!
So: let your pretty head be bowed,
Like a stricken flower, upon my knee;
And when you come to the sweet, sweet word
Of *best*, my little one — my bird,
Say it over twice, and say it loud.
I do not dare to lift my eyes

To our meek Master in the skies ;
For it was my wicked pride, alas !
That brought me to the heavy pass
Of weary waiting aud listening sad
To the winds as they drearily drift and drive·
So pray in your praying for me, my lad !
Oh ! if he were there in the chair you set,
With never a silvery fish in his net,
I'd be the happiest woman alive !

But he will come ere long, I know:
Here, Johnny, put your hand in mine,
And climb up to my shoulder — so :
Upon the cupboard's highest shelf
You'll see a bottle of good old wine —
I pressed the berry-juice myself,
Ah ! how it sparkles in the light,
To make us loth to break the seal ;
But though its warm red life could feel.
We would not spare it — not to-night !

Another hour ! and he comes not yet :
And I hear the long waves wash the beach,
With the moan of a drowning man in each,
And the star of hope is near to set.
The proudest lady in all the land
That sits in her chamber fine and high,
That sits in her chamber large and grand,
I would not envy to-night — not I —
If I had his cold wet locks in my hand,
To make them warm and to make them dry,
And to comb them with my fingers free
From the clinging sea-weed and the sand
Washing over them, it may be.

Ah! how should I envy the lady fair
With white arms hidden in folds of lace,
If my dear old fisher were sitting there,
His pipe in his hand, and his sun-brown face
Turning this way and that to me,
As I broiled the salmon and steeped the tea.
O empty heart! and O empty chair!
My boy, my Johnny, say over your prayer;
And straight to the words I told you keep,
Till you pass the best man out on the deep,
And then say this: If thou grantest, Lord,
That he come back alive, and with fish in his net,
The church shall have them for her award,
And we, of our thankfulness, will set
A day for fasting and scourge and pain.
Hark! hark to the crazy winds again!
The tide is high as high can be,
The waters are boiling over the bar,
And drawing under them near and far
The low black land.   Ah me! ah me!
I can only think of the mad, mad sea;
I can only think, and think, and think
How quickly a foundered boat would sink,
And how soon the stoutest arms would fail.
'Tis all of my worry and all of my fret,
For I brewed the bitter draught I drink:
I teased for a foolish, flimsy veil,
And teased and teased for a spangled gown,
And to have a holiday in the town.
There was only just one way, one way,
And he mended his net and trimmed his sail,
And trusted his life to the pitiless sea,
My dear old fisher, for love of me,

When a better wife would have said him nay;
And so my folly forlorn I bewail.
Hark! Midnight! All the hearth is dim
And cold; but sure we need not strive
To keep it warm and bright for him —
He never will come back alive.
I hear the creak of masts a-strain,
As the mad winds rush madly on.
Kneel down and say yet once again
The prayer I told you a while ago;
And be not loud, my boy, my John —
Nay, it befits us to be low —
Nor yet so straight to the wording keep,
As I did give you charge before:
The best man ever was on the deep
Pray for; and say the best twice o'er.
But when through our blessèd Redeemer you say
The sweet supplication for him that's away,
That saints bring him back to us savèd from ill,
Add this to the Father: If so be Thy will.
And I, lest again my temptation assail,
Will yield to my chast'ning, and cover up head
With blackness of darkness, instead of the veil
I pined for in worry and pined for in fret,
Till my good man was fain to be gone with his net
Where but the winds scolded. Now get from your
      knees,
For I, from the depths of contrition, have said
The Amen before you. And we'll to the seas:
Belike some kind wave may be washing ashore,
With coils of rope and salt sea-weed, some sign
To be as a letter sent out of the brine
To tell us the last news — to say if he struck

On the rocks and went down — but hush! breathe not
    my lad.
O sweet Lord of Mercy! my brain is gone mad!
Or that was the tune that he whistles for luck!
Run! run to the door! open wide — wider yet!
He is there! — he is here! and my arms are outspread
I am clasping and kissing his hands rough and brown.
Are you living? or are you the ghost of my dead?
'Tis all of my worry and all of my fret;
Ashamed in his bosom I hung down my head.
He has been with his fishes to sell in the town,
For I see, snugly wrapt in the folds of his net,
The hindering veil and the spangled new gown.

MAID AND MAN.

ALL in the gay and golden weather,
    Two fair travellers, maid and man,
Sailed in a birchen boat together,
    And sailed the way that the river ran:
The sun was low, not set, and the west
Was colored like a robin's breast.

The moon was moving sweetly o'er them.
    And her shadow, in the waves afloat,
Moved softly on and on before them
    Like a silver swan, that drew their boat;
And they were lovers, and well content,
Sailing the way the river went.

And these two saw in her grassy bower,
  As they sailed the way the river run,
A little, modest, slim-necked flower
  Nodding and nodding up to the sun,
And they made about her a little song
And sung it as they sailed along:

" Pull down the grass about your bosom,
  Nor look at the sun in the royal sky,
'Tis dangerous, dangerous, little blossom,
  You are so low, and he is so high —
'Tis dangerous nodding up to him,
He is so bright, and you are so dim ! "

Sweetly over, and sadly under,
  They turned the tune as they sailed along,
And they did not see the cloud, for a wonder,
  Break in the water, the shape of the swan ;
Nor yet, for a wonder, see at all
The river narrowing toward the fall.

" Be warned, my beauty — 'tis not the fashion
  Of the king to wed with the waiting-maid —
Wake not from sleep his fiery passion,
  But turn your red cheek into the shade —
The dew is a-tremble to kiss your eyes —
And there is but danger in the skies ! "

Close on the precipice rang the ditty,
  But they looked behind them, and not before,
And went down singing their doleful pity
  About the blossom safe on the shore —
" There is danger, danger ! frail one, list ! "
Backward whirled in the whirling mist.

CRADLE SONG.

ALL by the sides of the wide wild river
  Surging sad through the sodden land,
There be the black reeds washing together —
  Washing together in rain and sand ;
Going, blowing, flowing together —
  Rough are the winds, and the tide runs high —
Hush little babe in thy silken cradle —
  Lull lull, lull lull, lull lullaby !

Father is riding home, little baby,
  Riding home through the wind and rain ;
Flinty hoofs on the flag stems beating
  Thrum like a flail on the golden grain.
All in the wild, wet reeds of the lowlands,
  Dashed and plashed with the freezing foam
There be the blood-red wings of the starlings
  Shining to light and lead him home.

Spurring hard o'er the grass-gray ridges —
  Slacking rein in the low, wet land,
Where be the black reeds washing together —
  Washing together in rain and sand.
Down of the yellow-throated creeper —
  Plumes of the woodcock, green and black —
Boughs of salix, and combs of honey —
  These be the gifts he is bearing back.

Yester morning four sweet ground-doves
  Sung so gay to their nest in the wall —
Oh, by the moaning, and oh, by the droning,
  The wild, wild water is over them all !

Come, O morning, come with thy roses,
  Flame like a burning bush in the sky —
Hush, little babe, in thy silken cradle —
  Lull lull, lull lull, lull lullaby!

THE DOUBLE SKEIN.

Up ere the throstle is out of the thorn,
  Or the east a-blush with a rosy break,
For she wakens earlier now of a morn;
  Earlier now than she used to wake,
  Such troublous moanings the sea-waves make.

She leans to her distaff a weary brow,
  And her cheeks seem ready the flax to burn,
And the wheel in her hand turns heavier now;
  Heavier now than it used to turn,
  When strong hands helped her the bread to earn.

She lists to the school-boy's laugh and shout,
  And her eyes have the old expectant gleam;
And she draws the fine thread out and out,
  Till it drags her back from her tender dream,
  And wide and homeless the world doth seem.

Over the fields to the sands so brown,
  And over the sands to the restless tides
She looks, and her heart tilts up and down;
  Up and down with the boat as it rides,
  And she cries, " God steady the hand that guides!"

She watches the lights from the sea-cliffs go,
  Bedazed with a wonder of vague surprise,
For the sun seems now to be always low,
  And never to rise as he used to rise —
  The gracious glory of land and skies.

She shrinks from the pattered plash of the rain,
  For it taps not now as it used to do,
Like a tearful Spirit of Love at the pane,
  And the gray mist sweeping across the blue
  Never so lightly, chills her through.

So spins she ever a double skein,
  And the thread on her finger all eyes may see,
But the other is spun in her whirling brain
  And out of the sea-fog over the sea,
  For still with its treasure the heart will be.

SELFISH SORROW.

The house lay snug as a robin's nest
  Beneath its sheltering tree,
And a field of flowers was toward the west,
  And toward the east the sea,
Where a belt of weedy and wet black sand
Was always pushing in to the land.

And with her face away from the sun
  And toward the sea so wild,
The grandam sat, and spun and spun,
  And never heeded the child,

So wistfully waiting beside her chair,
More than she heeded the bird of the air

Fret and fret, and spin and spin,
   With her face the way of the sea :
And, whether the tide were out or in,
   A-sighing, " Woe is me ! "
In spite of the waiting and wistful eyes
Pleading so sweetly against the sighs.

And spin, spin, and fret, fret,
   ,And at last the day was done,
And the light of the fire went out and met
   The light o' the setting sun.
" It will be a stormy night — ah me ! "
Sighed the grandam, looking at the sea.

" Oh, no, it isn't a-going to rain ! "
   Cries the dove-eyed little girl,
Pressing her cheek to the window-pane
   And pulling her hair out of curl.
But the grandam answered with a sigh,
Just as she answered the cricket's cry,

" If it rains, let it rain ; we shall not drown ! "
   Says the child, so glad and gay ;
"The leaves of the aspen are blowing down ;
   A sign of fair weather, they say ! "
And the grandam moaned, as if the sea
Were beating her life out, " Woe is me ! "

The heart of the dove-eyed little girl
   Began in her throat to rise,

And she says, pulling golden curl upon curl
  All over her face and her eyes,
" I wish we were out of sight of the sea ! "
And the grandam answered, " Woe is me ! "

The sun in a sudden darkness slid,
  The winds began to plain,
And all the flowery field was hid
  With the cold gray mist and the rain.
Then knelt the child on the hearth so low,
And blew the embers all aglow.

On one small hand so lily white
  She propped her golden head,
And lying along the rosy light
   She took her book and read :
And the grandam heard her laughter low,
As she rocked in the shadows to and fro.

At length she put her spectacles on
  And drew the book to her knee :
" And does it tell," she said, "about John,
  My lad, who was lost at sea ? "
" Why, no," says the child, turning face about,
" 'Tis a fairy tale : shall I read it out ? "

The grandam lowlier bent upon
  The page as it lay on her knee :
" No, not if it doesn't tell about John,"
  She says, " who was lost at sea."
And the little girl, with a saddened face,
Shut her hair in the leaves to keep the place.

2

And climbing up and over the chair,
  The way that her sweet heart led,
She put one arm, so round and fair,
  Like a crown, on the old gray head.
"So, child," says the grandam — keeping on
  With her thoughts — "your book doesn't tell about
    John?"

"No, ma'am, it tells of a fairy old
  Who lived in a daffodil bell,
And who had a heart so hard and cold
  That she kept the dews to sell;
And when a butterfly wanted a drink,
  How much did she ask him, do you think?"

"O foolish child, I cannot tell,
  May be a crown, or so."
"But the fairy lived in a daffodil bell,
  And couldn't hoard crowns, you know!"
And the grandam answered — her thought joined on
  To the old thought — "Not a word about John?"

"But, grandam" — "Nay, for pity's sake
  Don't vex me about your crown,
But say if the ribs of a ship should break
  And the ship's crew all go down
Of a night like this, how long it would take
  For a strong-limbed lad to drown!"

"But, grandam" — "Nay, have done," she said,
  "With your fairy and her crown!
Besides, your arm upon my head
  Is heavy; get you down!"

"O ma'am, I'm so sorry to give you a pain!"
And the child kissed the wrinkled face time and again.

And then she told the story through
  Of the fairy of the dell,
Who sold God's blessed gift of the dew
  When it wasn't hers to sell,
And who shut the sweet light all away
With her thick black wings, and pined all day.

And how at last God struck her blind.
  The grandam wiped a tear,
And then she said, "I shouldn't mind
  If you read to me now, my dear!"
And the little girl, with a wondering look,
Slipped her golden hair from the leaves of the book.

As the grandam pulled her down to her knee,
  And pressed her close in her arm,
And kissing her, said, "Run out and see
  If there isn't a lull in the storm!
I think the moon, or at least some star,
Must shine, and the wind grows faint and far."

Next day again the grandam spun,
  And oh, how sweet were the hours!
For she sat at the window toward the sun,
  And next the field of flowers,
And never looked at the long gray sea,
Nor sighed for her lad that was lost, "Ah me!"

THE EDGE OF DOOM.

HEART-SICK, homeless, weak, and weary,
　On the edge of doom she stands,
Fighting back the wily Tempter
　With her trembling woman's hands.
On her lip a moan of pleading,
　In her eyes a look of pain,
Men and women, men and women,
　Shall her cry go up in vain?

On the edge of doom and darkness —
　Darker, deeper than the grave —
Off with pride, that devil's virtue!
　While there yet is time to save.
Clinging for her life, and shrinking
　Lower, lower from your frown:
Men and women, men and women,
　Will you, can you, crowd her down?

On that head, so early faded,
　Pitiless the rains have beat;
Famine down the pavements tracked her
　By her bruised and bleeding feet.
Through the years, sweet old Naomi,
　Lead her in the gleaners' way;
Boaz, oh, command your young men
　To reproach her not, I pray.

Face to face with shame and insult
　Since she drew her baby-breath,
Were it strange to find her knocking
　At the cruel door of death?

Were it strange if she should parley
  With the great arch-fiend of sin?
Open wide, O gates of mercy,
  Wider, wider! — let her in!

Ah! my proud and scornful lady,
  Lapped in laces fair and fine,
But for God's good grace and mercy
  Such a fate as her's were thine.
Therefore, breaking combs of honey,
  Breaking loaves of snowy bread,
If she ask a crumb, I charge you
  Give her not a stone instead.

Never lullaby, sung softly,
  Made her silken cradle stir;
Never ring of gay young playmates
  Opened to make room for her!
Therefore, winds, sing up your sweetest,
  Rocking lightly on the leaves;
And, O reapers, careless reapers,
  Let her glean among your sheaves!

Never mother, by her pillow,
  Knelt and taught her how to say,
Lead me not into temptation,
  Give me daily bread this day.
Therefore, reapers, while the corn-stalks
  To your shining sickles lean,
Drop, oh drop some golden handfuls —
  Let her freely come and glean!

Never mellow furrows crumbled
  Softly to her childish tread —

She but sowed in stony places,
 And the seed is choked and dead.
Therefore, let her rest among you
 When the sunbeams fiercely shine —
Barley reapers, let her with you
 Dip her morsel in the wine!

And intreat her not to leave you
 When the harvest week is o'er,
Nor depart from following after,
 Even to the threshing-floor.
But when stars through fields of shadow
 Shepherd in the evening gray,
- Fill her veil with beaten measures,
 Send her empty not away.

Then the city round about her,
 As she moveth by, shall stir
As it moved to meet Naomi
 Home from famine — yea, for her!
And the Lord, whose name is Mercy,
 Steadfast by your deed shall stand,
And shall make her even as Rachel,
 Even as Leah, to the land.

THE CHOPPER'S CHILD.

A STORY FOR THANKSGIVING DAY.

THE smoke of the Indian Summer
  Darkened and doubled the rills,
And the ripe corn, like a sunset,
  Shimmered along the hills;
Like a gracious glowing sunset,
  Inlaced with the rainbow light
Of vanishing wings a-trailing
  And trembling out of sight;

As, with the brier-buds gleaming
  In her darling, dimpled hands,
Toddling slow adown the sheep-paths
  Of the yellow stubble-lands —
Her sweet eyes full of the shadows
  Of the woodland, darkly brown —
Came the chopper's little daughter,
  In her simple hood and gown.

Behind her streamed the splendors
  Of the oaks and elms so grand,
Before her gleamed the gardens
  Of the rich man of the land;
Gardens about whose gateways
  The gloomy ivy swayed,
Setting all her heart a-tremble
  As she struck within their shade.

Now the chopper's lowly cabin
  It lay nestled in the wood,

And the dwelling of the rich man
  By the open highway stood,
With its pleasant porches facing
  All against the morning hills,
And each separate window shining
  Like a bed of daffodils.

Up above the tallest poplars
  In its stateliness it rose,
With its carved and curious gables,
  And its marble porticoes ;
But she did not see the grandeur,
  And she thought her father's oaks
Were finer than the cedars
  Clipt so close along the walks.

So, in that full confiding
  The unworldly only know,
Through the gateway, down the garden,
  Up the marble portico,
Her bare feet brown as becs' wings,
  And her hands of brier-buds full,
On, along the fleecy crimson
  Of the carpets of dyed wool,

With a modest glance uplifted
  Through the lashes drooping down,
Came the chopper's little daughter,
  In her simple hood and gown ;
Still and steady, like a shadow
  Sliding inward from the wood,
Till before the lady-mistress
  Of the house, at last, she stood.

Oh, as sweet as summer sunshine
  Was that lady-dame to see,
With the chopper's little daughter,
  Like a shadow at her knee !
Oh, green as leaves of clover
  Were the broideries of her train,
And her hand it shone with jewels
  Like a lily with the rain.

And the priest before the altar,
  As she swam along the aisle,
Reading out the sacred lesson,
  Read it consciously, the while ;
The long roll of the organ
  Drew across a silken stir,
And when he named a saint, it was
  As if he named but her.

But the chopper's child undazzled
  In her lady-presence stood —
(She was born amid the splendors
  Of the glorious autumn wood) —
And so sweetly and serenely
  Met the cold and careless face,
Her own alive with blushes,
  E'en as one who gives a grace :

As she said, the accents falling
  In a pretty, childish way :
" To-morrow, then to-morrow
  Will have brought Thanksgiving day ;
And my mother will be happy,
  And be honored, so she said,

To have the landlord's lady
  Taste her honey and her bread."

Then slowly spake the lady,
  As disdainfully she smiled,
" Live you not in yonder cabin ?
  Are you not the chopper's child?
And your foolish mother bids me
  To Thanksgiving, do you say ?
What is it, little starveling,
  That you give your thanks for, pray ? "

One bashful moment's silence —
  Then hushing up her pain,
And sweetness growing out of it
  As the rose does out of rain —
She stript the woolen kerchief
  From off her shining head,
As one might strip the outer husk
  From the golden ear, and said :

" What have we to give thanks for ?
  Why, just for daily bread ! "
And then, with all her little pride
  A-blushing out so red —
" Perhaps, too, that the sunshine
  Can come and lie on our floor,
With none of your icy columns
  To shut it from the door ! "

" What have we to give thanks for ? '
  And a smile illumed her tears,
As a star the broken vapors,
  When it suddenly appears ;

And she answered, all her bosom
   Throbbing up and down so fast:
" Because my poor sick brother
   Is asleep at last, at last.

" Asleep beneath the daisies :
   But when the drenching rain
Has put them out, we know the dew
   Will light them up again ;
And we make and keep Thanksgiving
   With the best the house affords,
Since, if we live, or if we die,
   We know we are the Lord's :

" That out of his hands of mercy
   Not the least of us can fall ;
But we have ten thousand blessings,
   And I cannot name them all !
Oh, see them yourself, good madame —
   I will come and show you the way —
After the morrow, the morrow again
   Will be the great, glad day."

And, tucking up her tresses
   In the kerchief of gray wool,
Where they gleamed like golden woodlights
   In the autumn mists so dull,
She crossed the crimson carpets,
   With her rose-buds in her hands,
And, climbing up the sheep-paths
   Of the yellow stubble-lands,

Passed tne marsh wherein the starlings
   Shut so close their horny bills,

And lighted with her loveliness
The gateway of the hills.
Oh, the eagle has the sunshine,
　And his way is grand and still;
But the lark can turn the cloud into
A temple when she will!

That evening, when the cornfields
　Had lost the rainbow light
Of vanishing wings a-trailing
　And trembling out of sight,
Apart from her great possessions
　And from all the world apart,
Knelt the lady-wife and mistress
　Of the rich man's house and heart.

Knelt she, all her spirit broken,
　And the shame she could not speak,
Burning out upon the darkness
　From the fires upon her cheek;
And prayed the Lord of the harvest
　To make her meek and mild,
And as faithful in Thanksgiving
　As the chopper's little child.

THE DEAD-HOUSE.

In the dead of night to the Dead-house,
　She cometh — a maiden fair —
By the feet so slight and slender,
By the hand so white and tender,

And by the silken and shining lengths
 Of the girlish, golden hair,
  Dragging under and over
The arms of the men that bear.
  Oh! make of your pity a cover,
And softly, silently bear :
  Perhaps for the sake of a lover,
Loved all too well, she is there!

In the dead of night to the Dead-house!
 So lovely and so lorn —
  Straighten the tangled tresses,
  They have known a mother's kisses,
And hide with their shining veil of grace
The sightless eyes and the pale, sad face
  From men and women's scorn.
 Aye, veil the poor face over,
  And softly, silently bear :
  Perhaps for the sake of a lover,
  Loved all too well, she is there.

In the dead of night to the Dead-house!
 Bear her in from the street :
  The watch at his watching found her —
  Ah! say it low nor wound her,
For though the heart in the bosom
 Has ceased to throb and beat,
Speak low, when you say how they found her
 Buried alive in the sleet.
Speak low, and make her a cover
 All out of her shining hair :
Perhaps for the sake of a lover,
 Loved all too well, she was there.

Desolate left in the Dead-house!
  Your cruel judgments spare,
  Ye know not why she is there :
Be slow to pronounce your " *mene,*"
Remember the Magdalene ;
  Be slow with your harsh award —
Remember the Magdalene ;
  Remember the dear, dear Lord !
Holy, and high above her,
  By the length of her sin and shame,
He could take her and love her —
  Praise to his precious name.

With oil of gentle mercy
  The tide of your censure stem ;
Have ye no scarlet sinning ?
No need for yourselves of winning
Those sweetest words man ever spake
In all the world for pity's sake,
Those words the hardest heart that break :
" Neither do I condemn."

In the light of morn to the Dead-house
  There cometh a man so old —
" My child ! " he cries ; " I will wake her ;
Close, close in my arms I will take her,
And bear her back on my shoulder,
  My poor stray lamb to the fold !
How came she in this dreadful place? "
And he stoops and puts away from the face
  The queenly cover of gold.
" No, no ! " he says, " it is not my girl ! "
As he lifts the tresses curl by curl,
  " She was never so pale and cold ! "

In the light of morn in the Dead-house,
  He prattleth like a child —
" No, no ! " he says, " it cannot be —
Her sweet eyes would have answered me,
  And her sweet mouth must have smiled —
She would have asked for her mother,
And for the good little brother
  That thought it pastime and pleasure
To be up and at work for her.
And she doth not smile nor stir."
And then, with his arms outspread
From the slender feet to the head,
  He taketh the fearful measure.
" No, no ! " he says, " she would wake and smile " —
But he listens breathless all the while
  If haply the heart may beat,
And tenderly with trembling hands
Out of the shining silken bands
  Combs the frozen sleet.

In the light of morn in the Dead-house,
  He prattleth on and on —
" As like her mother's as can be
These two white hands ; but if 'twere she
  Who out of our house is gone,
I must have found here by her side
He to whom she was promised bride ;
And yet this way along the sleet
We tracked the little wandering feet.
And yesterday, her mother said,
When she waked and called her from her bed,
She looked like one a dream had crazed —
Her mother thought the sunshine dazed,

And thought it childish passion
That made her, when she knelt to pray,
Falter, and be afraid to say,
  Lord, keep us from temptation.
And I bethink, the mother said —
(What puts such thoughts into my head?)
  That never once the live-long day
  Her darling sung the old love-lay
That 'twas her use to sing and hum
  As hums the bee to the blossom:
And that when night was nearly come
  She took from its place in her bosom
The picture worn and cherished long,
And as if that had done her wrong,
    Or, as if in sudden ire,
And it were something to abhor,
  She laid it, not as she used at night
Among the rose-leaves in the drawer,
  But out of her bosom and out of sight
    With its face against the fire.

" But why should I torment my heart
  (And the tear from his cheek he dashes)
As if such thoughts had any part
  With these pale, piteous ashes ? "
He opens the lids, and the eyes are blue,
" But these are frost and my child's were dew !
    No, no ! it is not my poor lost girl."
  And he takes the tresses curl by curl
    And tenderly feels them over.
  " If it were she, the watch I know
    Would never have dragged her out of the snow —
      Why, where should be her lover ! "

And down the face and bosom fair
He spread the long loose flood of hair,
And left her in the Dead-house there,
All under her queenly cover.

ONE MOMENT.

ONE moment, to strictly run out by the sands —
  Time, in the old way just to say the old saying —
  Enough for your giving — enough for my playing
The hope of a life in your sinless white hands —
  To call you my sweetheart, and ask you to be
  My fond little fairy and live by the sea !

Five minutes — ten — twenty ! but little to spare,
  Yet enough to repeat, in the homely old fashion,
  A story of true love, unfrenzied with passion —
To say, " Will you make my rough weather be fair,
  And give me each day your red cheek to be kissed ?
  My dear one, my darling, my rose of the mist ? "

An half hour ! — would I dare say longer yet —
  And the time (is so much you will yield to my
    wishes).
  When luck-thriven fishermen draw their last fishes,
Whose silver sleek sides in the sea dripping net,
  And speckles of red gold, and scales thin and crisp,
  Through the fog-drizzle shine like a Will-o'-the-wisp.

An hour ! nay more — until star after star
  Takes his watch while the west-wind through shadows
    thick falling,

Holds parley, in moans, with the tide, outward
   crawling,
And licking the long shaggy back of the bar,
   As if in lamenting some ship gone aground,
   Or sailor, love-lorn, in the dead waters drowned.

Two hours! and not a hair's breadth from the grace
   Of your innocent trust would I any more vary
   Than rob of her lilies the virginal Mary;
But just in my two hands would hold your fair face,
   And look in your dove-eyes, and ask you to be
   My good little housewife, and live by the sea!

Till midnight! till morning! old Time has fleet wings,
   And the space will be brief, so my courage to steady,
   As say, " Who weds me may not be a fine lady
With silk gowns to wear, and twenty gold rings,
   But with only a nest in the rocks, leaving me
   Her praises to sing as I sail on the sea."

I would buy her a wheel, and some flax-wisps, and wool,
   So when the wild gusts of the winter were blowing,
   And poor little bird-nest half hid in the snowing,
The time never need to be dreary nor dull —
   But smiling the brighter. the darker the day,
   Her sunshine would scatter the shadows away.

At eve, when the mist, like a shawl of fine lace,
   Wrapt her softly about, like a queen in her splendor,
   She still would sing over old sea-songs, so tender,
To keep her in mind of her sailor's brown face —
   Of his distance and danger, and make her to be
   His good little housewife content by the sea.

Believe me, sweet sweetheart, they have but hard lives
  Who go down to sea in great ships, never knowing
  How soon cruel waves o'er their heads will be flowing
And fatherless children, and true-hearted wives,
  The place of their dead never see, never know —
  But the nest waits, my darling, ah ! say, will you go ?

THE FLAX-BEATER.

" Now give me your burden, if burden you bear,"
      So the flax-beater said,
" And press out and wring out the rain from your hair,
      And come into my shed ;
  The sweetest sweet-milk you shall have for your fare,
      And the whitest white-bread,
  With a sheaf of the goldenest straw for your bed ;
  Then give me your burden, if burden you bear,
      And come into my shed !

" I make bold to press my poor lodging and fare,
      For the wood-path is lone,
  Aye, lonely and dark as a dungeon-house stair,
      And jagged with stone.
  Sheer down the wild hills, and with thorn-brush o'er-
      grown,
  I have lost it myself in despite of my care,
  Though I'm used to rough ways and have courage to
      spare ;
  And then, my good friend, if the truth must be known,
  The huts of the settlers that stand here and there
      Are as rude as my own.

" The night will be black when the day shall have gone ;
  'Tis the old of the moon,
And the winds will blow stiff, and more stiffly right on,
  By the cry of the loon ;
Those terrible storm-harps, the oaks, are in tune,
That creaking will fall to a crashing anon ;
For the sake of your pitiful, poor little one,
You cannot, good woman, have lodging too soon !

" Hark ! thunder ! and see how the waters are piled,
  Cloud on cloud, overhead ;
Mayhap I'm too bold, but I once had a child —
  Sweet lady, she's dead —
The daffodil growing so bright and so wild
  At the door of my shed
Is not yet so bright as her glad golden head,
And her smile ! ah, if you could have seen how she
  smiled !
But what need of praises — you too have a child ! "
  So the flax-beater said.

" Ah, the soft summer-days, they were all just as one,
  And how swiftly they sped ;
When the daisy scarce bent to her fairy-like tread,
And the wife, as she sat at her wheel in the sun,
Sang sea-songs and ditties of true-love that run
  All as smooth as her thread ;
When her darling was gone then the singing was done,
And she sewed her a shroud of the flax she had spun,
  And a cap for her head.

" See that cloud running over the last little star,
  Like a great inky blot,

And now, in the low river hollows afar,
You can hear the wild waters through driftwood and
        bar,
    Boil up like a pot;
It is as if the wide world was at war,
So give me your burden, if such you have got,
And come to my shed, for you must, will or not."

" Get gone, you old man ! I've no burden to bear ;
    You at best are misled !
And as for the rain, let it fall on my hair ;
    Is that so much to dread,
That I should be begging for lodging and fare
    At a flax-beater's shed ?
Get gone, and have done with your insolent stare,
And keep your gold straw, if you leave me instead
    But the ground for my bed ! "
'Twas thus the strange woman with wringing wet hair
    In her wretchedness said.

" No burden ! and what is it then that I trace
    Wrapt so close in your shawl ?
I remember the look of the dear little face,
And remember the look of the head, round and small,
    That I saw once for all
Under thin, filmy folds, like the folds of your shawl ! "
" Why, then, 'tis my bride-veil and gown, have the grace
To believe — they are rolled in my kerchief of lace ;
    And that, old man, is all ! "

" Woman ! woman ! bethink what it is that you say,
    Lest it bring you to harm.
A bride-veil and gown are not hid such a way
    As the thing in your arm ! "

"My good man, my dear man, remember, I pray,
    What trifles were sacred your own wedding day,
    And leave me my bride-veil and gown hid away
        From the fret of the storm.
    Oh, soften your heart to accept what I say —
    It is these, only these that I have in my arm!"

' Only these! just a touch of this thing, and I know
        That my thoughts were misled!
    But why turn you pale? and why tremble you so?
        If it be as you said,
    You have nothing from me nor from mortal to dread.'
    Her voice fell to sobs, and she hung down her head,
    Hugged his knees, kissed his hands, kissed his feet as
            she said :
" Now spare me, oh spare me this death-dealing blow,
    And give me your cold, coldest pity, instead ;
    I was crazed, and I spake you a lie in my woe :
        I am bearing my dead,
    To bury it out of my sight, you must know ;
        But, good and sweet sir, I am wed, I am wed!"

" Unswathe you the corpse, then, and give it to me,
        If that all be so well ;
    But what are these slender blue marks that I see
        At the throat?   Can you tell?"
" The kisses I gave it as it lay on my knee!"
" And dare you, false woman, to lie so to me?"
        " Why, then 'twas the spell
    And work of a demon that came out of hell."
" Now God give you mercy, if mercy there be,
        For the angels that fell,
    Because, if there came up a demon from hell.
        That demon was thee!"

COTTAGE AND HALL.

With eyes to her sewing-work dropped down.
  And with hair in a tangled shower,
And with roses kissed by the sun, so brown,
  Young Janey sat in her bower —
A garden nook with work and book ;
  And the bars that crossed her girlish gown
Were as blue as the flaxen flower.
  And her little heart it beat and beat,
Till the work shook on her knee,
  For the golden combs are not so sweet
To the honey-fasting bee
  As to her her thoughts of Alexis.

And across a good green piece of wood,
  And across a field of flowers,
A modest, lowly house there stood
  That held her eyes for hours —
A cottage low, hid under the snow
  Of cherry and bean-vine flowers.
Sometimes it held her all day long,
  For there at her distaff bent,
And spinning a double thread of song
  And of wool, in her sweet content,
Sat the mother of young Alexis.

And Janey turned things in and out,
  As foolish maids will do.
What could the song be all about ?
  Yet well enough she knew

That while the fingers drew the wool
  As fine as fine could be,
The loving mother-heart was full
  Of her boy gone to sea —
Her blue-eyed boy, her pride and joy,
  On the cold and cruel sea —
Her darling boy, Alexis.

And beyond the good green piece of wood,
  And the field of flowers so gay,
Among its ancient oaks there stood,
  With gables high and gray,
A lofty hall, where mistress of all
  She might dance the night away.
And as she sat and sewed her seam
  In the garden bower that day
Alike from seam and alike from dream
  Her truant thoughts would stray ;
It would be so fine like a lady to shine,
  And to dance the night away !
And oh and alas for Alexis !

And suns have risen and suns gone down
  On cherry and bean-vine bowers,
And the tangled curls o'er the eyes dove-brown
  They fall no more in showers ;
Nor are there bars in the homespun gown
  As blue as the flaxen flowers.
Aye, winter wind and winter rain
  Have beaten away the bowers,
And little Janey is Lady Jane,
  And dances away the hours !
Maidens she hath to play and sing,
  And her mother's house and land

Could never buy the jeweled ring
   She wears on her lily hand —
The hand that is false to Alexis!

Ah, bright were the sweet young cheeks and eyes,
   And the silken gown was gay,
When first to the hall as mistress of all
   She came on her wedding-day.
" Now where, my bride," says the groom in pride —
   " Now where will your chamber be ? "
And from wall to wall she praises all,
   But chooses the one by the sea!
And the suns they rise and the suns they set,
   But she rarely sees their gleam,
For often her eyes with tears are wet,
   And the sewing-work is unfinished yet,
And so is the girlish dream.

For when her ladies gird at her,
   And her lord is cold and stern,
Old memories in her heart must stir,
   And she cannot choose but mourn
For the gentle boy, Alexis!

And alway, when the dance is done,
   And her weary feet are free,
She sits in her chamber all alone
   At the window next the sea,
And combs her shining tresses down
   By the light of the fading stars,
And may be thinks of her homespun gown
   With the pretty flax-flower bars.
For when the foam of wintry gales
   Runs white along the blue,

Hearing the rattle of stiffened sails,
 She trembles through and through,
And may be thinks of Alexis.

THE MINES OF AVONDALE.

OLD Death proclaims a holocaust —
 Two hundred men must die !
And he cometh not like a thief in the night,
 But with 'banners lifted high.
He calleth the North wind out o' th' North
 To blow him a signal blast,
And to plough the air with a fiery share,
 And to sow the sparks, broadcast.
No fear hath he of the arm of flesh,
 And he maketh the winds to cry,
Let come who will to this awful hill
 And his strength against me try !

So quick those sparks along the land
 Into blades of flame have sprung ;
So quick the piteous face of Heaven
 With a veil of black is hung :
And men are telling the news with words,
 And women with tears and sighs,
And the children with the frightened souls
 That are staring from their eyes.
"Death, death is holding a holocaust !
 And never was seen such pyre —
Head packed to head and above them spread
 Full forty feet of fire ! "

From hill to hill-top runs the cry.
   Through farm and village and town,
And high and higher — " The mine's on fire!
   Two hundred men sealed down!
And not with the dewy hand o' th' earth,
   And not with the leaves of the trees —
Nor is it the waves that roof their graves —
   Oh no, it is none of these —
From sight and sound walled round and round —
   For God's sake haste to the pyre!
In the black coal-beds, and above their heads
   Full forty feet of fire! "

And now the villages swarm like bees,
   And the miners catch the sound,
And climb to the land with their picks in hand
   From their chambers in the ground.
For high and low and rich and poor,
   To a holy instinct true,
Stand forth as if all hearts were one
   And a-tremble through and through.
On, side by side they roll like a tide,
   And the voice grows high and higher,
" Come woe, come weal, we must break the seal
   Of that forty feet of fire! "

Now cries of fear, shrill, far and near,
   And a palsy shakes the hands,
And the blood runs cold, for behold, behold
   The gap where the enemy stands!
Oh, never had painter scenes to paint
   So ghastly and grim as these —
Mothers that comfortless sit on the ground
   With their babies on their knees:

The brown cheeked lad and the maid as sad
    As the grandame and the sire,
And 'twixt them all and their loved, that wall —
    That terrible wall of fire!

And the grapple begins and the foremost set
    Their lives against death's laws,
And the blazing timbers catch in their arms
    And bear them off like straws.
They have lowered the flaunting flag from its place —
    They will die in the gap, or save;
For this they have done, whate'er be won —
    They have conquered fear of the grave.
They have baffled — have driven the enemy,
    And with better courage strive;
" Who knoweth," they say, " God's mercy to-day,
    And the souls He may save alive!"

So now the hands have digged through the brands —
    They can see the awful stairs,
And there falls a hush that is only stirred
    By the weeping women's prayers.
" Now who will peril his limb and life,
    In the damps of the dreadful mine?"
" I, I, and I!" a dozen cry,
    As they forward step from line!
And down from the light and out o' th' sight,
    Man after man they go,
And now arise th' unanswered cries
    As they beat on the doors below.

And night came down — what a woeful night!
    To the youths and maidens fair,

What a night in the lives of the miners' wives
 At the gate of a dumb despair.
And the stars have set their solemn watch
 In silence o'er the hill,
And the children sleep and the women weep,
 And the workers work with a will.
And so the hours drag on and on,
 And so the night goes by,
And at last the east is gray with dawn,
 And the sun is in the sky.

Hark, hark ! the barricades are down,
 The torchlights further spread,
The doubt is past — they are found at last —
 Dead, dead ! two hundred dead !
Face, close to face, in a long embrace,
 And the young and the faded hair —
Gold over the snow as if meant to show
 Love stayed beyond despair.
Two hundred men at yester morn
 With the work of the world to strive ;
Two hundred yet when the day was set,
 And not a soul alive !

Oh, long the brawny Plymouth men,
 As they sit by their winter fires,
Shall tell the tale of Avondale
 And its awful pyre of pyres.
Shall hush their breath and tell how Death
 His flag did wildly wave,
And how in shrouds of smoky clouds
 The miners fought in their graves.

And how. in a still procession
   They passed from that fearful glen,
And there shall be wail in Avondale,
   For the brave two hundred men.

THE VICTORY OF PERRY.

SEPTEMBER 10TH, 1813.

LIFT up the years ! lift up the years,
   Whose shadows around us spread ;
Let us tribute pay to the brave to-day
   Who are half a century dead.   ·

Oh, not with tears — no, not with tears,
   The grateful nation comes,
But with flags out-thrown, and bugles blown,
   And the martial roll of drums !

Beat up, beat up ! till memory glows
   And sets our hearts aflame !
Ah, they did well in the fight who fell,
   And we leave them to their fame ;

Their fame, that larger, grander grows
   As time runs into the past,
For the Erie-waves chant over their graves,
   And shall, while the world shall last.

O beautiful cities of the Lake,
   As ye sit by your peaceful shore,

Make glad and sing till the echoes ring,
For our brave young Commodore!

He knew your stormy oaks to take
And their ribs into ships contrive,
And to set them so fine in battle line,
With their timbers yet alive.[1]

We see our squadron lie in the Bay
Where it lay so long ago,
And hear the cry from the mast-head high,
Three times, and three, " *Sail ho!* "

Through half a century to-day
We hear the signal of fight —
" *Get under way!   Get under way!*
The enemy is in sight ! "

Our hearts leap up — our pulses thrill,
As the boatswains' pipes of joy
So loudly play o'er the dash o' the spray,
" *All hands up anchor ahoy!* "

Now all is still, aye, deathly still ;
The enemy's guns are in view !
" *To the royal fore!* " cries the Commodore,
And up run the lilies and blue.[2]

---

[1] Perry, it will be remembered, cut down the trees, built and launched the ships of his fleet, all within three months.

[2] The famous fighting flag was inscribed with the immortal words of the dying Lawrence, in large white letters on a blue ground, legible throughout the squadron.

And hark to the cry, the great glad cry, —
   All a-tremble the squadron stands —
From lip to lip, " *Don't give up the ship !* "
   And then " *To quarters, all hands !* "

An hour, an awful hour drags by —
   There's a shot from the enemy's gun !
" *More sail ! More sail ! Let the canister hail !* "
   Cries Perry, and forward, as one,

Caledonia, Lawrence, and Scorpion, all
   Bear down and stand fast, till the flood
Away from their track sends the scared billows back
   With their faces bedabbled in blood.

The Queen [1] and her allies their broadsides let fall —
   Oh, the Lawrence is riddled with storms —
Where is Perry ? afloat ! he is safe in his boat
   And his battle-flag up in his arms !

The bullets they hiss and the Englishmen shout —
   Oh, the Lawrence is sinking, a wreck —
But with flag yet a-swing like a great bloody wing
   Perry treads the Niagara's deck !

With a wave of his hand he has wheeled her about —
   Oh, the nation is holding its breath —
Headforemost he goes in the midst of his foes
   And breaks them and rakes them to death !

And lo, the enemy, after the fray,
   On the deck that his dead have lined,

[1] *Queen Charlotte* of the British line.

With his sword-hilt before to our Commodore
  And his war-dogs in leash behind !

And well, the nation does well to-day,
  Setting her bugles to blow,
And her drums to beat for the glorious fleet
  That humbled her haughty foe.

Ah, well to come with her autumn flowers,
  A tribute for the brave
Who died to make our Erie Lake
  Echo through every wave —

" *We've met the enemy and they're ours !* "
  And who died, that we might stand,
A country free and mistress at Sea
  As well as on the Land.

THE WINDOW JUST OVER THE STREET.

I SIT in my sorrow a-weary, alone ;
  I have nothing sweet to hope or remember,
For the spring o' th' year and of life has flown ;
  'Tis the wildest night o' the wild December,
  And dark in my spirit and dark in my chamber.

I sit and list to the steps in the street,
  Going and coming, and coming and going,
And the winds at my shutter they blow and beat ;
  'Tis the middle of night and the clouds are snowing ;
  And the winds are bitterly beating and blowing.

4

I list to the steps as they come and go,
　And list to the winds that are beating and blowing,
And my heart sinks down so low, so low ;
　　No step is stayed from me by the snowing,
　　Nor stayed by the wind so bitterly blowing.

I think of the ships that are out at sea,
　Of the wheels in th' cold, black waters turning. ;
Not one of the ships beareth news to me,
　　And my head is sick, and my heart is yearning,
　　As I think of the wheels in the black waters turning.

Of the mother I think, by her sick baby's bed,
　Away in her cabin as lonesome and dreary,
And little and low as the flax-breaker's shed ;
　　Of her patience so sweet, and her silence so weary,
　　With cries of the hungry wolf hid in the prairie.

I think of all things in the world that are sad ;
　Of children in homesick and comfortless places ;
Of prisons, of dungeons, of men that are mad ;
　　Of wicked, unwomanly light in the faces
　　Of women that fortune has wronged with disgraces.

I think of a dear little sun-lighted head,
　That came where no hand of us all could deliver ;
And crazed with the cruelest pain went to bed
　　Where the sheets were the foam-fretted waves of the
　　　river ;
　　Poor darling ! may God in his mercy forgive her.

The footsteps grow faint and more faint in the snow ;
　I put back the curtain in very despairing ;

The masts creak and groan as th' winds come and go ;
  And the light in the light-house all weirdly is flaring
But what glory is this, in the gloom of despairing !

I see at the window just over the street,
  A maid in the lamplight her love-letter reading.
Her red mouth is smiling, her news is so sweet ;
  And the heart in my bosom is cured of its bleeding.
  As I look on the maiden her love-letter reading.

She has finished the letter, and folding it, kisses,
  And hides it — a secret too sacred to know ;
And now in the hearth-light she softly undresses :
  A vision of grace in the roseate glow,
  I see her unbinding the braids of her tresses.

And now as she stoops to the ribbon that fastens
  Her slipper, they tumble o'er shoulder and face ;
And now, as she patters in bare feet, she hastens
  To gather them up in a fillet of lace ;
  And now she is gone, but in fancy I trace

The lavendered linen updrawn, the round arm
  Half sunk in the counterpane's broidered roses,
Revealing the exquisite outline of form ;
  A willowy wonder of grace that reposes
  Beneath the white counterpane, fleecy with roses.

I see the small hand lying over the heart,
  Where the passionate dreams are so sweet in their
      sally ;
The fair little fingers they tremble and part,

As part to th' warm waves the leaves of the lily,
And they play with her hand like the waves with the
　　lily.

In white fleecy flowers, the queen o' the flowers!
　What to her is the world with its bad, bitter weather?
Wide she opens her arms — ah, her world is not ours!
　And now she has closed them and clasped them
　　together —
　What to her is our world, with its clouds and rough
　　weather?

Hark! midnight! the winds and the snows blow and
　　beat;
　I drop down the curtain and say to my sorrow,
Thank God for the window just over the street;
　Thank God there is always a light whence to borrow,
　When darkness is darkest, and sorrow most sorrow.

PITILESS FATE.

I saw in my dream a wonderful stream,
　And over the stream was a bridge so slender,
And over the white there was scarlet light,
　And over the scarlet a golden splendor.

And beyond the bridge was a goodly ridge
　Where bees made honey and corn was growing,
And down that way through the gold and gray
　A gay young man in a boat was rowing,

I could see from the shore that a rose he wore
  Stuck in his button-hole, rare as the rarest,
And singing a song and rowing along,
  I guessed his face to be fair as the fairest.

And all by the corn where the bees at morn
  Made combs of honey — with breathing bated,
I saw by the stream (it was only a dream)
  A lovely lady that watched and waited.

There were fair green leaves in her silken sleeves,
  And loose her locks in the winds were blowing,
And she kissed to land with her milk-white hand
  The gay young man in the boat a-rowing.

And all so light in her apron white
  She caught the little red rose he cast her,
And, " Haste ! " she cried, with her arms so wide,
  " Haste, sweetheart, haste ! " but the boat was past her

And the gray so cold ran over the gold,
  And she sighed with only the winds to hear her —
" He loves me still, and he rowed with a will,
  But pitiless Fate, not he, was steerer ! "

And there till the morn blushed over the corn
  And over the bees in their sweet combs humming,
Her locks with the dew drenched through and through
  She watched and waited her false love's coming !

But the maid to-day who reads my lay
  May keep her young heart light as a feather —
It was only a dream, the bridge and the stream,
  And lady and lover, and all together.

A FABLE OF CLOUD-LAND.

Two clouds in the early morning
  Came sailing up the sky —
'Twas summer, and the meadow-lands
  Were brown and baked and dry.

And the higher cloud was large and black,
  And of a scornful mind,
And he sailed as though he turned his back
  On the smaller one behind.

At length, in a voice of thunder,
  He said to his mate so small,
" If I wasn't a bigger cloud than you,
  I wouldn't be one at all ! "

And the little cloud that held her place
  So low along the sky,
Grew red, then purple, in the face,
  And then she began to cry !

And the great cloud thundered out again
  As loud as loud could be,
" Lag lowly still, and cry if you will,
  I'm going to go to sea !

" The land don't give me back a smile,
  I will leave it to the sun,
And will show you something worth your while,
  Before the day is done ! "

So off he ran, without a stop,
   Upon his sea voyage bent,
And he never shed a single drop
   On the dry land as he went.

And directly came a rumble
   Along the air so dim;
And then a crash, and then a dash,
   And the sea had swallowed him!

"I don't make any stir at all,"
   Said the little cloud, with a sigh,
And her tears began like rain to fall
   On the meadows parched and dry.

And over the rye and the barley
   They fell and fell all day,
And soft and sweet on the fields of wheat,
   Till she wept her heart away.

And the bean-flowers and the buckwheat
   They scented all the air,
And in the time of the harvest
   There was bread enough and to spare.

I know a man like that great cloud
   As much as he can live,
And he gives his alms with thunder-cloud
   Where there is no need to give.

And I know a woman who doth keep
   Where praise comes not at all,
Like the modest cloud that could but weep
   Because she was so small.

The name of the one the poor will bless
When her day shall cease to be,
And the other will fall as profitless
As the cloud did in the sea.

BARBARA AT THE WINDOW.

CLOSE at the window-pane Barbara stands;
 The walls o' th' dingy old house are aglow;
Pressing her cheeks are her two little hands,
 Drooping her eyelids so meek and so low.

What do you see, little Barbara? Say!
 The walls o' th' dingy old house are aglow;
The leaves they are down, and the birds are away,
 And lilac and rosebush are white with the snow.

An hour the sun has been out o' th' west;
 The walls o' th' poor little house are aglow;
Come, Barbara, come to th' hearth with th' rest,
 Right gayly she tosses her curls for a " No ! "

The grandmother sits in her straw-bottom chair;
 And rafter and wall they are brightly aglow;
The dear little mother is knitting a pair
 Of scarlet-wool stockings tipt white at th' toe.

A glad girl and boy are at play by her knee;
 The walls o' th' poor little house are aglow !
Now driving th' crickets, for cows, in their glee,
 Now rolling the yarn-balls o' scarlet and snow.

And now they are fishers, with nets in the stream ;
  And rafter and wall o' the house are aglow ;
Or sleeping, or waking, their lives are a dream ;
  But what seeth Barbara, there in the snow ?

And th' voice of Barbara ringeth out clear ;
  The walls, the rough rafters, how brightly they glow
If you will believe me, I see you all here !
  Our dear little room seemeth double, you know.

The fire, the tea-kettle swung on the crane ;
  And rafter and wall with the candle aglow ;
Grandmother and mother, right over again !
  And Peter, and Katherine, all in the snow.

Sweet Barbara, standing so close to th' pane,
  With the walls o' th' little house brightly aglow ;
You will only see everything over again,
  Whatever you see, and wherever you go !

BARBARA IN THE MEADOW.

THE morn is hanging her fire-fringed veil,
  Made of the mist, o'er the walnut boughs,
And Barbara, with her cedar pail,
  Comes to the meadow to call the cows.

" The little people that live in the air
  Are not for my human hands to wrong,"
Says Barbara, and her loving prayer
  Takes them up as it goes along.

Gay sings the miller, and Barbara's mouth
   Purses with echoes it will not repeat,
And the rose on her cheek hath a May-day's growth
   In the line with the ending, " I love you, sweet."

Yonder the mill is, small and white,
   Hung like a vapor among the rocks —
Good spirits say to her morn and night,
   " Barbara, Barbara! stay with your flocks."

Stay for the treasures you have to keep,
   Cherish the love that you know is true;
Though stars should shine in the tears you weep,
   They never would come out of heaven to you.

And were you to follow the violet veins
   Over the hills — to the ends of the earth,
Barbara, what would you get for your pains,
   More than your true-love's love is worth?

So, never a thought about braver mills,
   Of prouder lovers your dreaming cease;
A world is shut in among these hills —
   Stay in it, Barbara, stay, for your peace!

BALLAD OF UNCLE JOE.

WHEN I was young — it seems as though
   There never were such when —
There lived a man that now I know
   Was just the best of men;

I'll name him to you, " Uncle Joe,"
    For so we called him then.

A poor man he, that for his bread
    Must work with might and main.
The humble roof above his head
    Scarce kept him from the rain ;
But so his dog and he were fed,
    He sought no other gain.

His steel-blue axe, it was his pride,
    And over wood and wave
Its music rang out far and wide,
    His strokes they were so brave ;
Excepting that some neighbor died,
    And then he dug his grave.

And whether it were wife or child,
    An old·man, or a maid,
An infant that had hardly smiled,
    Or youth, so lowly laid,
The yellow earth was always piled
    Above them by his spade.

For spade he had, and grubbing-hoe,
    And hence the people said
It was not much that Uncle Joe
    Should bury all the dead ;
So rich and poor, and high and low,
    He made them each a bed.

The funeral-bell was like a jog
    Upon his wits, they say,

That made him leave his half-cut log
  At any time of day,
And whistle to his brindle dog
  And light his pipe of clay.

When winter winds around him drave
  And made the snow-flakes spin,
I've seen him — for he did not save
  His strength, for thick nor thin —
His bare head just above the grave
  That he was standing in.

His simple mind was almost dark
  To school-lore, that is true;
The wisdom he had gained at work
  Was nearly all he knew;
But ah, the way he made his mark
  Was honest, through and through

'Twas not among the rulers then
  That he in council sat;
They used to say that with his pen
  His fingers were not pat;
But he was still a gentleman
  For all and all of that.

The preacher in his silken gown
  Was not so well at ease
As he, with collar lopping down
  And patches at his knees,
The envy of our little town,
  He hadn't a soul to please;

Nor wife nor brother, chick nor child,
  Nor any kith nor kin.
Perhaps the townsfolk were beguiled
  And the envy·was a sin,
Bnt his look of sweetness when he smiled
  Betokened joy within.

He sometimes took his holiday,
  And 'twas a pleasant sight
To see him smoke his pipe of clay,
  As if all the world went right,
While his brindle dog beside him lay
  A-winking at the light.

He took his holiday, and so
  His face with gladness shone;
But, ah! I cannot make you kuow
  One bliss he held alone,
Unless the heart of Uncle Joe
  Were beating in your own!

He had an old crackèd violin,
  And I just may whisper you
The music was so weak and thin
  'Twas like to an ado,
As he drew the long bow out and in
  To all the tune he knew.

From January on till June,
  And back again to snow,
Or in the tender light o' the moon,
  Or by the hearth-fire's glow,
To that old-fashioned, crazy tune
  He made his elbow go!

Ah! then his smile would come so sweet
　　It brightened all the air,
And heel and toe would beat and beat
　　Till the ground of grass was bare,
As if that little lady feet
　　Were dancing with him there!

His finger nails, so bruised and flat,
　　Would grow in this employ
To such a rosy roundness that
　　He almost seemed a boy,
And even the old crape on his hat
　　Would tremble as with joy.

So, digging graves, and chopping wood,
　　He spent the busy day,
And always, as a wise man should,
　　Kept evil thoughts at bay;
For when he could not speak the good,
　　He hadn't a word to say.

And so the years in shine and storm
　　Went by, as years will go,
Until at last his palsied arm
　　Could hardly draw the bow;
Until he crooked through all his form,
　　Much like his grubbing-hoe.

And then his axe he deeply set,
　　And on the wall-side pegs
Hung hoe and spade; no fear nor fret
　　That life was at the dregs,
But walked about of a warm day yet,
　　With his dog between his legs.

Sometimes, as one who almost grieves,
  His memory would recall
The merry-making Christmas-eves,
  The folic, and the ball,
Till his hands would shake like withered leaves
  And his pipe go out and fall.

Then all his face would grow as bright —
  So I have oft heard say —
As if that, being lost in the night,
  He saw the dawn o' the day ;
As if from a churlish, chilling height
  He saw the light o' the May.

One winter night the fiddle-bow
  His fingers ceased to tease,
And they found him by the morning glow
  Beneath his door-yard trees,
Wrapt in the ermine of the snow,
  And royally at ease.

What matter that the winds were wild ?
  He did not hear their din,
But hugging, as it were his child,
  Against his grizzly chin,
The treasure of his life, he smiled,
  For all was peace within.

And when they drew the vest apart
  To fold the hands away
They found a picture past all art
  Of painting, so they say ;
And they turned the face upon the heart,
  And left it where it lay.

And one, a boy with golden head,
  Made haste and strung full soon
The crazy viol; for he said,
  Mayhap beneath the moon
They danced sometime a merry tread
  To the belovèd tune.

And many an eye with tears was dim
  The while his corse they bore;
No hands had ever worked for him
  Since he was born before;
Nor could there come an hour so grim
  That he should need them more.

The viol, ready tuned to play,
  The sadly-silent bow,
The axe, the pipe of yellow clay,
  Are in his grave so low;
And there is nothing more to say
  Of poor old Uncle Joe.

POEMS OF THOUGHT.

SUPPLICATION.

DEAR gracious Lord, if that thy pain
   Doth make me well, if I have strayed
   Past mercy, let my hands be laid
One in the other ; not in vain
   Would I be dressed, Lord, in the beauteous clay
   Which thou did'st put away.

But if thou yet canst find in me
   A vine, though trailing on the ground,
   That might be straightened up, and bound
To any good, so let it be ;
   And, haply at the last, some tendril-ring
   Unto thy hand shall cling.

I have been too much used, I know,
   To tell my needs in fretful words.
   The clamoring of the silly birds,
Impatient for their wings to grow,
   Has thy forgiveness ; O my blessed Lord,
   The like to me accord.

Of grace, as much as will complete
   Thy will in me, I pray thee for ;
   Even as a rose shut in a drawer,
That maketh all about it sweet,
   I would be, rather than the cedar, fine,
   Help me, thou Power divine.

5

Fill thou my heart with love as full
  As any lily with the rain ;
  Unteach me ever to complain,
And make my scarlet sins as wool ;
  Yea, wash me, even with sorrows, clean and fair,
  As lightnings do the air.

PLEDGES.

SOMETIMES the softness of the embracing air,
  The tender beauty of the grass and sky,
The look of still repose the mountains wear,
  The sea-waves that beside each other lie
Contented in the sun — the flowery gleams
  Of gardens by the doors of cottages,
The sweet, delusive blessedness of dreams,
  The pleasant murmurs of the forest trees
Clinging to one another — all I see,
  And hear, and all that fancy paints,
Do touch me with a deep humility,
  And make me be ashamed of my complaints.
Then, in my meditations, I resolve
  That I will never, while I live, again
Ruffle the graceful ministries of love
  With brows distrustful, or with wishes vain.
Then I make pledges to my heart and say
  We two will live serener lives henceforth ;
For what is all the outward beauty worth,
  The golden opening of the sweetest day
That ever shone, if we arise to hide,   .
  Not from ourselves, but from men's eyes away,
The last night's petulance unpacified !

HER voice was sweet and low ; her face
  No words can make appear,
For it looked out of heaven but long enough   .
  To leave a shadow here.

And I only knew that I saw the face,
  And saw the shadow fall,
And that she carried my heart away,
  And keeps it ; that is all.

PROVERBS IN RHYME.

TIME makes us eagle-eyed :
  Our fantasies befriend us in our youth,
And build the shadowy tents wherein we hide
  Out of the glare of truth.

Make no haste to despise
  The proud of spirit : ofttimes pride but is
An armor worn to shield from insolent eyes
  Our human weaknesses.

Be slow to blame his course
  Or name him coward who disdains to fight :
Courage is just a blind impelling force,
  And often wrong as right.

Condemn not her whose hours
  Are not all given to spinning nor to care :
Has not God planted every path with flowers
  Whose end is to be fair ?

Think not that he is cold
  Who runneth not your proffered hand to touch :
On feeling's heights 'tis wise the step to hold
  From trembling overmuch ;

And though its household sweets
  Affection may through daily channels give,
The heart is chary, and ecstatic beats
  Once only while we live.

FAME.

Fame guards the wreath we call a crown
  With other wreaths of fire,
And dragging this or that man down
  Will not raise you the higher !
Fear not too much the open seas,
  Nor yet yourself misdoubt ;
Clear the bright wake of geniuses,
  Then steadily steer out.
That wicked men in league should be
  To push your craft aside,
Is not the hint of modesty,
  But the poor conceit of pride.

GENIUS.

A cunning and curious splendor,
  That glorifies commonest things —
Palissy, with clay from the river,
  Moulds cups for the tables of kings.

A marvel of sweet and wise madness,
 That passes our skill to define;
It clothes the poor peasant with grandeur,
 And turns his rude hut to a shrine.

Full many a dear little daisy
 Had passed from the light of the sun,
Ere Burns, with his pen and his ploughshare,
 Upturned and immortalled *that* one.

And just with a touch of its magic
 It gives to the poet's rough rhyme
A *something* that makes the world listen,
 And will, to the ending of time.

It puts a great price upon shadows —
 Holds visions, all rubies above,
And shreds of old tapestries pieces
 To legends of glory and love.

The ruin it builds into beauty,
 Uplifting the low-lying towers,
Makes green the waste place with a garden,
 And shapes the dead dust into flowers.

It shows us the lovely court ladies,
 All shining in lace and brocade;
The knights, for their gloves who did battle,
 In terrible armor arrayed.

It gives to the gray head a glory,
 And grace to the eyelids that weep,
And makes our last enemy even,
 To be as the brother of sleep.

A marvel of madness celestial,
　　That causes the weed at our feet,
The thistle that grows at the wayside,
　　To somehow look strange and be sweet.

No heirs hath it, neither ancestry ;
　　But just as it listeth, and when,
It seals with its own royal signet
　　The foreheads of women and men.

IN BONDS.

WHILE shines the sun, the storm even then
　　Has struck his bargain with the sea —
Oh, lives of women, lives of men,
　　How pressed, how poor, how pinched ye be !

It is as if, having granted power
　　Almost omnipotent to man,
Heaven grudged the splendor of the dower,
　　And going back upon her plan,

Mortised his free feet in the ground,
　　Closed him in walls of ignorance,
And all the soul within him bound
　　In the dull hindrances of sense.

Hence, while he goads his will to rise,
　　As one his fallen ox might urge,
The conflict of the impatient cries
　　Within him wastes him like a scourge.

Even as dreams his days depart,
　His work no sure foundation forms,
Immortal yearnings in his heart,
　And empty shadows in his arms!

It is as if, being come to land,
　Some pestilence, with fingers black,
Loosed from the wheel the master hand
　And drove the homesick vessel back;

As if the nurslings of his care
　Chilled him to death with their embrace;
As if that she he held most fair
　Turned round and mocked him to his face

And thus he stands, and ever stands,
　Tempted without and torn within;
Ashes of ashes in his hands,
　Famished and faint, and sick with sin.

Seeing the cross, and not the crown;
　The o'erwhelming flood, and not the ark;
Till gap by gap his faith throws down
　Its guards, and leaves him to the dark.

And when the last dear hope has fled,
　And all is weary, dreary pain,
That enemy, most darkly dread,
　Grows pitiful, and snaps the chain.

NOBILITY.

TRUE worth is in *being*, not *seeming*, —
  In doing each day that goes by
Some little good — not in the dreaming
  Of great things to do by and by.
For whatever men say in blindness,
  And spite of the fancies of youth,
There's nothing so kingly as kindness,
  And nothing so royal as truth.

We get back our mete as we measure —
  We cannot do wrong and feel right,
Nor can we give pain and gain pleasure,
  For justice avenges each slight.
The air for the wing of the sparrow,
  The bush for the robin and wren,
But alway the path that is narrow·
  And straight, for the children of men.

'Tis not in the pages of story
  The heart of its ills to beguile,
Though he who makes courtship to glory
  Gives all that he hath for her smile.
For when from her heights he has won her,
  Alas ! it is only to prove
That nothing's so sacred as honor,
  And nothing so loyal as love !

We cannot make bargains for blisses,
  Nor catch them like fishes in nets ;
And sometimes the thing our life misses,
  Helps more than the thing which it gets.

For good lieth not in pursuing,
  Nor gaining of great nor of small,
But just in the doing, and doing
  As we would be done by, is all.

Through envy, through malice, through hating,
  Against the world, early and late,
No jot of our courage abating —
  Our part is to work and to wait.
And slight is the sting of his trouble
  Whose winnings are less than his worth ;
For he who is honest is noble,
  Whatever his fortunes or birth.

TO THE MUSE.

PHANTOMS come and crowd me thick,
  And my heart is sick, so sick ;
Kindness no more refresh
Brain nor body, mind nor flesh.
Good Muse, sweet Muse, comfort me
With thy heavenly company.

Thieves beset me on my way,
Day and night and night and day,
Stealing all the lovely light
That did make my dreams so bright.
Good Muse, sweet Muse, hide my treasures
High among immortal pleasures.

Friendship's watch is weary grown,
And I lie alone, alone ;

Love against me flower-like closes,
Blushing, opening toward the roses.
Good Muse, sweet Muse, keep my friend
To the sad and sunless end.

Oh, the darkness of the estate
Where I, stript and bleeding, wait,
Torn with thorns and with wild woe,
In my house of dust so low !
Good Muse, sweet Muse, make my faith
Strong to triumph over death.

Rock me both at morns and eves
In a cradle lined with leaves —
Light as winds that stir the willows
Stir my hard and heavy pillows.
Good Muse, sweet Muse, rock me soft,
Till my thoughts soar all aloft.

Seal my eyes from earthly things
With the shadow of thy wings,
Fill with songs the wildering spaces,
Till I see the old, old faces,
Rise forever, on forever —
Good Muse, sweet Muse, leave me never.

NO RING.

WHAT is it that doth spoil the fair adorning
  With which her body she would dignify,
When from her bed she rises in the morning
  To comb, and plait, and tie
Her hair with ribbons, colored like the sky ?

What is it that her pleasure discomposes
  When she would sit and sing the sun away —
Making her see dead roses in red roses,
    And in the downfall gray
A blight that seems the world to overlay ?

What is it makes the trembling look of trouble
  About her tender mouth and eyelids fair ?
Ah me, ah'me ! she feels her heart beat double,
    Without the mother's prayer,
And her wild fears are more than she can bear.

To the poor sightless lark new powers are given,
  Not only with a golden tongue to sing,
But still to make her wavering way toward heaven
    With undiscerning wing ;
But what to her doth her sick sorrow bring ?

Her days she turns, and yet keeps overturning,
  And her flesh shrinks as if she felt the rod ;
For 'gainst her will she thinks hard things concerning
    The everlasting God,
And longs to be insensate like the clod.

Sweet Heaven, be pitiful ! rain down upon her
  The saintly charities ordained for such ;
She was so poor in everything but honor,
    And she loved much — loved much !
Would, Lord, she had thy garment's hem to touch.

Haply, it was the hungry heart within her,
  The woman's heart, denied its natural right,

That made her the thing men call sinner,
   Even in her own despite :
Lord, that her judges might receive their sight !

TEXT AND MORAL.

FULL early in that dewy time of year
   When wheat and barley fields are gay and green,
And when the flag uplifts his dull gray spear,
   And cowslips in their yellow coats are seen,
And every grass-tuft by the common ways
Holdeth some red-mouthed flower to give it praise :

Just as the dawn was at that primal hour
   That brings such tender golden sweetness in,
Ere yet the sun had left his eastern bower
   And set upon the hills his rounded chin,
I heard a little song — three notes — not more —
Plained like a low petition at my door.

And all that day and other days I heard
   The same low-asking note, and then I found
My beggar in the likeness of a bird.
   Surely, I said, she hideth some deep wound
Under the speckled beauty of her wing,
That she doth seem to rather cry than sing.

Haply some treacherous man, and evil-eyed,
   Hath spoiled her nest or snared her lovely mate ;
But while I spoke, a bird unharmed I spied
   High in the elm-top, all his heart elate,

And splitting with its joy his shining bill,
Unmindful of that low, sad " trill-a-trill ! "

At sunset came my boys with cheeks ablush,
   And fairly flying on their arms and legs,
To tell that they had found within a bush
   A bird's-nest, lined with little rose-leaf eggs !
Then, inly musing, I renewed my quest
Knowing that no bird singeth on her nest.

And still, the softest morns, the sweetest eves,
   And when from out the midnight, blue and still,
The tender moon looked in between the leaves,
   That little, plaining, pleading trill-a-trill !
Would tremble out, and fall away, and fade,
And so I mused and mused, until I made

A text at last of the melodious cry,
   And drew this moral (was it fetched too far ?)
Life's inequalities so underlie
   The things we have, so rest in what we are,
That each must steadfast to his nature keep,
And one must soar and sing, and one must weep.

TO MY FRIEND.

If we should see one sowing seed
   With patient care and toil and pain,
Then to some other garden speed
   And sow again ;

And so right on from day to day,
  And so right on through months and years,
Watering the furrows all the way
    With rain of tears;

Ne'er gladdened by the yellowing top
  Of harvest, nor of ripened rose,
Till suddenly the plough should stop, —
    The work-day close;

Should we not, as the day ran by,
  Wonder to see him take no ease,
And cry at nightfall, " Vanity
    Of Vanities!"

And yet 'tis thus, my friend, the hours
  And days go by, with you and me.
We, too, are sowing seeds of flowers
    We never see.

Sometimes we sow in soil of sin;
  Sometimes where choking thorns abound;
And sometimes cast our good seed in
    Dry, stony ground.

Our stalks spring up and fade and die
  Under the burning noontide heat,
And hopes and plans about us lie
    All incomplete;

And as the toilsome days go by
  Unrespited with flowery ease,
Angels may cry out, " Vanity
    Of Vanities!"

Oh, when, fruitionless, the night
   Descends upon our day of ills,
   God grant we find our harvests white
    On heavenly hills. '

ONE OF MANY.

BECAUSE I have not done the things I know
   I ought to do, my very soul is sad ;
   And furthermore, because that I have had
Delights that should have made to overflow
   My cup of gladness, and have not been glad.

All in the midst of plenty, poor I live ;
   My house, my friend, with heavy heart I see,
   As if that mine they were not meant to be ;
For of the sweetness of the things I have
   A churlish conscience dispossesses me.

I do desire, nay, long, to put my powers
   To better service than I yet have done —
   Not hither, thither, without purpose run,
And gather just a handful of the flowers,
   And catch a little sunlight of the sun.

Lamenting all the night and all the day
   Occasion lost, and losing in lament
   The golden chances that I know were meant
For wiser uses — asking overpay
   When nothing has been earned, and all was lent.

Keeping in dim and desolated ways,
   And where the wild winds whistle loud and shrill
   Through leafless bushes, and the birds are still,
And where the lights are lights of other days —
   A sad insanity o'ermastering will.

And saddest of the sadness is to know
   It is not fortune's fault, but only mine,
   That far away the hills of roses shine —
And far away the pipes of pleasure blow —
   That we, and not our stars, our fates assign.

LIGHT.

BE not much troubled about many things,
Fear often hath no whit of substance in it,
   And lives but just a minute ;
While from the very snow the wheat-blade springs.
   And light is like a flower,
That bursts in full leaf from the darkest hour.
   And He who made the night,
Made, too, the flowery sweetness of the light.
Be it thy task, through his good grace, to win it.

TRUST.

SOMETIMES when hopes have vanished, one and all,
   Soft lights drop round about me in their stead,
As if there had been cast across Heaven's wall
   Handfuls of roses down upon my bed ;
Then through my darkness pleasures come in crowds,
Shining like larks' wings in the sombre clouds,

And I am fed with sweetness, as of dew
  Strained through the leaves of pansies at day dawn;
But not the flowery lights that overstrew
  The bed my weary body rests upon,
Is it that maketh all my house so bright,
And feedeth all my soul with such delight.

Nay, ne'er could heavenly, veritable flowers
  Make the rude time to run so smoothly by,
And tie with amity the alien hours,
  As might some maiden, with her ribbon, tie
A bunch of homely posies into one,
Making all fair, when none were fair alone.

But lying disenchanted of my fear,
  'Neath the gold borders of my " coverlid "
So overstrown, I feel my flesh so near
  Things lovely, that, my body being hid
Out of the sunshine, shall not harm endure,
But mix with daisies, and grow fair and pure.

Oh, comfortable thought! yet not of this
  Get I the peace that drieth all my tears;
For, wrapped within this truth, another is
  Sweeter and stronger to dispel my fears:
If through its change my flesh shall death defy,
Surely my soul shall not be left to die.

Our God, who taketh knowledge of the flowers,
  Making our bodies change to things so fine,
Knoweth the insatiate longings that are ours,
  For fadeless blooms and suns that alway shine.
His name is Love, and love can work no ill;
Hence, though He slay me, I will trust Him still.

LIFE.

Solitude — Life is inviolate solitude —
 Never was truth so apart from the dreaming.
 As lieth the selfhood inside of the seeming,
Guarded with triple shield out of all quest,
 So that the sisterhood nearest and sweetest,
 So that the brotherhood kindest, completest,
Is but an exchanging of signals at best.

Desolate — Life is so dreary and desolate —
 Women and men in the crowd meet and mingle,
 Yet with itself every soul standeth single,
Deep out of sympathy moaning its moan —
 Holding and having its brief exultation —
 Making its lonesome and low lamentation —
Fighting its terrible conflicts alone.

Separate — Life is so sad and so separate —
 Under love's ceiling with roses for lining,
 Heart mates with heart in a tender entwining,
Yet never the sweet cup of love filleth full —
 Eye looks in eye with a questioning wonder,
 Why are we thus in our meeting asunder?
Why are our pulses so slow and so dull?

Fruitless, fruitionless — Life is fruitionless —
 Never the heaped up and generous measure —
 Never the substance of satisfied pleasure —
Never the moment with rapture elate —
 But draining the chalice, we long for the chalice,
 And live as an alien inside of our palace,
Bereft of our title and deeds of estate.

Pitiful — Life is so poor and so pitiful —
   Cometh the cloud on the goldenest weather —
   Briefly the man and his youth stay together —
Falleth the frost ere the harvest is in,
   And conscience descends from the open aggression
   To timid and troubled and tearful concession,
And downward and down into parley with sin.

Purposeless — Life is so wayward and purposeless —
   Always before us the object is shifting,
   Always the means and the method are drifting,
We rue what is done — what is undone deplore —
   More striving for high things than things that are holy,
   And so we go down to the valley so lowly
Wherein there is work, and device never more.

Vanity, vanity — all would be vanity,
   Whether in seeking or getting our pleasures —
   Whether in spending or hoarding our treasures —
Whether in indolence, whether in strife —
   Whether in feasting and whether in fasting,
   But for our faith in the Love everlasting —
But for the life that is better than life.

PLEA FOR CHARITY.

IF one had never seen the full completeness
   Of the round year, but tarried half the way,
How should he guess the fair and flowery sweetness
   That cometh with the May —
Guess of the bloom, and of the rainy sweetness
   That come in with the May !

Suppose he had but heard the winds a-blowing,
  And seen the brooks in icy chains fast bound,
How should he guess that waters in their flowing
  Could make so glad a sound—
Guess how their silver tongues should be set going
  To such a tuneful sound !

Suppose he had not seen the bluebirds winging,
  Nor seen the day set, nor the morning rise,
Nor seen the golden balancing and swinging
  Of the gay butterflies—
Who could paint April pictures, worth the bringing
  To notice of his eyes?

Suppose he had not seen the living daisies,
  Nor seen the rose, so glorious and bright,
Were it not better than your far-off praises
  Of all their lovely light,
To give his hands the holding of the daisies,
  And of the roses bright?

O Christian man, deal gently with the sinner—
  Think what an utter wintry waste is his
Whose heart of love has never been the winner,
  To know how sweet it is —
Be pitiful, O Christian, to the sinner,
  Think what a world is his !

He never heard the lisping and the trembling
  Of Eden's gracious leaves about his head —
His mirth is nothing but the poor dissembling
  Of a great soul unfed —
Oh, bring him where the Eden-leaves are trembling,
  And give him heavenly bread.

As Winter doth her shriveled branches cover
  With greenness, knowing spring-time's soft desire,
Even so the soul, knowing Jesus for a lover,
  Puts on a new attire —
A garment fair as snow, to meet the Lover
  Who bids her come up higher.

SECOND SIGHT.

My thoughts, I fear, run less to right than wrong,
  And I am selfish, sinful, being human ;
But yet sometimes an impulse sweet and strong
  Touches my heart, for I am still a woman ;
And yesterday, beside my cradle sitting,
  And broidering lilies through my lullabies,
My heart stirred in me, just as if the flitting
  Of some chance angel touched me, and my eyes
Filled all at once to tender overflowing,
  And my song ended — breaking up in sighs ;
I could not see the lilies I was sewing
  For the hot tears, thick coming to my eyes.

The unborn years, like rose-leaves in a flame,
Shriveled together, and this vision came,
For I was gifted with a second seeing :
'Twas night, and darkly terrible with storms,
And I beheld my cherished darling fleeing
In all her lily broideries from my arms —
A babe no longer. Wild the wind was blowing,
And the snows round her soddened as they fell ;
And when a whisper told me she was going
That way wherein the feet take hold on hell,

I could not cry, I could not speak nor stir,
Held in mute torture by my love of her,

We make the least ado o'er greatest troubles ;
  Our very anguish doth our anguish drown ;
The sea forms only just a few faint bubbles
  Of stifled breathing when a ship goes down.

'Twas but a moment — then the merry laughter
  Of my sweet baby on the nurse's knee
  Rippled across the mists of fantasy ;
And sunshine, stretching like a golden rafter
  From cornice on to cornice o'er my head,
  Scattered the darkness, and my vision fled.

Times fall when Fate just misses of her blows,
  And, being warned, the victim slips aside ;
And thus it was with me — the idle shows,
  The foolish pomp of vanity and pride,
The work of cunning hands and curious looms,
Shining about my house like poppy-blooms,
  Like poppy-blooms had drowsed me, heart and
    brain ;
And all the currents of my blood were setting
  To that bad dullness that is worse than pain.
The moth will spoil the garment with its fretting
  Surer and faster than the work-day wear.
The quickening vision came — not all too late :
  I saw that there were griefs for me to share,
And the poor worldling missed the worldling's fate.

There was my baby — there was I, the mother,
  Broidering my lilies by the golden gleam

Of the glad suushine ; but was there no other
   Fleeing, as fled the phantom in my dream ?
Were there no hearts, because of their great loving,
Bound to the wheel of torture past all moving ?
   No storms of awful sorrow to be stemmed ?
   Yea, out of my own heart I stood condemned.

Leaving the silken splendor of my rooms,
   The sunshine stretching like a golden rafter
   From cornice on to cornice, and the laughter
Of my sweet baby on the nurse's knee,
Calling me back, and almost keeping me —
Leaving my windows bright with flowery blooms.
   I passed adown my broad emblazoned hall,
Along the soft mats, tufted thick across —
Scarlet and green, like roses grown with moss ;
   And parting from my pleasures, one and all,
Threaded my way through many a narrow street,
   From whose low cellars, lit with scanty embers,
Came great-eyed children, with bare, shivering feet,
   And wondered at me, through the doors gaped
     wide,
   Till they were crowded back, or pushed aside,
By some lean-elbowed man, or flabby crone,
Upon whose foreheads discontent had grown,
   As grows the mildew on decaying timbers.

"All thine is mine," came to me from the fall
   Of every beggar's footstep, and the glooms
That hung around held yet this other call :
"Who to himself lives only is not living ;
   He hath no gain who does not get by giving."
And so I came beneath the cold gray wall
   That shapes the awful prison of the Tombs.

Humility had been my gentle guide —
  I saw her not, a heavenly spirit she —
And when the fearful door swung open wide
  I heard her pleasant steps go in with me.

Oh for a tongue, and oh! for words to tell
  Of the young creature, masked with sinful guise,
That stood before me in her narrow cell
  And dragged my heart out with her pleading eyes.

I shook from head to foot, and could not stir —
Afraid, but not so much afraid of her
As of myself — made like her — of one dust,
And holding an immortal soul in trust
The same as she — perhaps not even so good,
Tempted with her temptations. Was't for me
To hold myself apart and call her sinner?
Not so; and silent, face to face we stood,
And as some traveller in the night belated
Waits for the star he knows must rise, so I
Patient within the prison darkness waited,
Trusting to see the better self within her
Rise from the ruins of her womanhood.

Nor did I wait in vain. At last, at last,
Her eager hand reached forth and held me fast,
  And drawing just a little broken breath,
As if she stood upon that narrow ground
  That lies a-tremble betwixt life and death.
Her yearning, fearful soul expression found:

" I'm dying — dying, and your dewy hand
  Is like the shadow to the sickly plant

Whose root is in the dry and burning sand.
   Pity, sweet pity — that is what I want.
You bring it — ah! you would not, if you knew."
I clasped her closer: " Friend, dear friend, I do! ·
   I know it all — from first to last," I said.
" 'Twas but a blind, mistaken search for good;
  ·Premeditated evil never led
To this sad end."   As one entranced she stood,
   And I went on : " Nay, but 'tis not the end :
God were not God if such a thing could be —
If not in time, then in eternity,
There must be room for penitence to mend
Life's broken chance, else noise of wars
Would unmake heaven.

                     The shadows of the bars
That darkened the poor face like devils' fingers
Faded away, and still in memory lingers
   The look of tender, tearful, glad surprise
   That brought the saint's soul to the sinner's eyes.

Life out of death ; it seemed to me as when
   The anchor, clutching, holds the driven ship,
   And to the cry scarce formed upon her lip,
" Lord God be praised! "   I answered with " Amen."

LIFE'S ROSES.

WHEN the morning first uncloses,
   And before the mists are gone,
All the hills seem bright with roses,
   Just a little farther on !

Roses red as wings of starlings,
   And with diamond dew-drops wet ;
" Wait," says Patience, " wait, my darlings —
   ·Wait a little longer yet ! "
So, with eager, upturned faces,
   Wait the children for the hours
That shall bring them to the places
   Of the tantalizing flowers.

Wild with wonder, sweet with guesses,
   Vexed with only fleeting fears ;
So the broader day advances,
   And the twilight disappears.
Hands begin to clutch at posies,
   Eyes to flash with new delight,
And the roses, oh ! the roses,
   Burning, blushing full in sight !

Now with bosoms softly heating,
   Heart in heart, and hand in hand,
Youths and maids together meeting
   Crowd the flowery harvest land.
Not a thought of rainy weather,
   Nor of thorns to sting and grieve,
Gather, gather, gather, gather,
   All the care is what to leave !

Noon to afternoon advances,
   Rosy red grows rus et brown ;
Sad eyes turn to backward glance ,
   So the sun of youth goes down.
And as rose by rose is withered,
   Sober sight begins to find

Many a false heart has been gathered,
　Many a true one left behind.
Hands are clasped with fainter holding,
　Unfilled souls begin to sigh
For the golden, glad unfolding
　Of the morn beyond the sky.

SECRET WRITING.

From the outward world about us,
　From the hurry and the din,
Oh, how little do we gather
　Of the other world within !
For the brow may wear upon it
　All the seeming of repose
When the brain is worn and weary,
　And the mind oppressed with woes :
And the eye may shine and sparkle
　As it were with pleasure's glow,
When 'tis only just the flashing
　Of the fires of pain below.
And the tongue may have the sweetness
　That doth seem of bliss a part,
When 'tis only just the tremble
　Of the weak and wounded heart.
Oh, the cheek may have the color
　Of the red rose, with the rest,
When 'tis only just the hectic
　Of the dying leaf, at best.

But when the hearth is kindled,
　And the house is hushed at night —
Ah, then the secret writing
　Of the spirit comes to light!
Through the mother's light caressing
　Of the baby on her knee,
We see the mystic writing,
　That she does not know we see —
By the love-light as it flashes
　In her tender-lidded eyes,
We know if that her vision rest
　·On earth, or in the skies;
And by the song she chooses,
　By the very tune she sings,
We know if that her heart be set
　On seen, or unseen things.

Oh, when the hearth is kindled —
　When the house is hushed — 'tis then
We see the hidden springs that move
　The open deeds of men.
As the father turns the lesson
　For the boy or girl to learn,
We perceive the inner letters ·
　That he knows not we discern.
For either by the deed he does,
　Or that he leaves undone,
We find and trace the channels
　Where his thoughts and feelings run.
And often as the unconscious act,
　Or smile, or word we scan,
Our hearts revoke the judgments
　We have passed upon the man.

Sometimes we find that he who says
    The least about his faith,
Has steadfastness and sanctity
    To suffer unto death ;
And find that he who prays aloud
    With ostentatious mien,
Prays only to be heard of men,
    And only to be seen.
For when the hearth is kindled,
    And the house is hushed at night —
Ah, then the secret writing
    Of the spirit comes to light.

DREAMS.

.Often I sit and spend my hour,
    Linking my dreams from heart to brain,
And as the child joins flower to flower,
    Then breaks and joins them on again,

Casting the bright ones in disgrace,
    And weaving pale ones in their stead,
Changing the honors and the place
    Of white and scarlet, blue and red ;

And finding after all his pains
    Of sorting and selecting dyes,
No single chain of all the chains
    The fond caprice that satisfies ;

So I from all things bright and brave,
    Select what brightest, bravest seems,
And, with the utmost skill I have,
    Contrive the fashion of my dreams.

Sometimes ambitious thoughts abound,
    And then I draw my pattern bold,
And have my shuttle only wound
    With silken threads, or threads of gold.

Sometimes my heart reproaches me,
    And mesh from cunning mesh I pull,
And weave in sad humility
    With flaxen threads or threads of wool.

For here the hue too brightly gleams,
    And there the grain too dark is cast,
And so no dream of all my dreams
    Is ever finished, first, or last.

And looking back upon my past
    Wronged with so many a wasted hour,
I think that I should fear to cast
    My fortunes if I had the power.

And think that he is mainly wise,
    Who takes what comes of good or ill,
Trusting that wisdom underlies
    And worketh in the end — His will.

MY POET.

AH, could I my poet only draw
In lines of a living light,
You would say that Shakespeare never saw
In his dreams a fairer sight.

Along the bright crisp grass where by
A beautiful water lay,
We walked — my fancies and I —
One morn in the early May.

And there, betwixt the water sweet
And the gay and grassy land,
I found the print of two little feet
Upon the silvery sand.

These following, and following on,
Allured by the place and time,
I, all of a sudden, came upon
This poet of my rhyme.

Betwixt my hands I longed to take
His two cheeks brown with tan,
To kiss him for my true love's sake,
And call him a little man.

A rustic of the rustics he,
By every look and sign,
And I knew, when he turned his face to me,
'Twas his spirit made him fine.

His ignorance he had sweetly turned
Into uses passing words :

He had cut a pipe of corn, and learned
  Thereon to talk to the birds.

And now it was the bluebird's trill,
  Now the blackbird on the thorn,
Now a speckle-breast, or twany-bill
  That answered his pipe of corn,

And now, though he turned him north and south,
  And called upon bird by bird,
There was never a little golden mouth
  Would answer him back a word.

For all, from the redbird bold and gay,
  To the linnet dull and plain,
Had fallen on beds of the leafy spray,
  To listen in envious pain.

" Ah, do as you like, my golden quill ; "
  So he said, for his wise share ;
" And the same to you, my tawny-bill,
  There are pleasures everywhere."

Then his heart fell in him dancing so,
  It spun to his cheek the red,
As he spied himself in the wave below
  A-standing on his head.

Ah, could I but his picture draw,
  Thus glad by his nature's right,
You would say that Shakespeare never saw
  In his dreams a fairer sight.

WRITTEN ON THE FOURTH OF JULY, 1864.

ONCE more, despite the noise of wars,
　And the smoke gathering fold on fold,
Our daisies set their stainless stars
　Against the sunshine's cloth of gold.

Lord, make us feel, if so thou will,
　The blessings crowning us to-day,
And the yet greater blessing still,
　Of blessings thou hast taken away.

Unworthy of the favors lent,
　We fell into apostasy ;
And lo! our country's chastisement
　Has brought her to herself, and thee !

Nearer by all this grief than when
　She dared her weak ones to oppress,
And played away her States to men
　Who scorned her for her foolishness.

Oh, bless for us this holiday,
　Men keep like children loose from school,
And put it in their hearts, we pray,
　To choose them rulers fit to rule.

Good men, who shall their country's pride
　And honor to their own prefer ;
Her sinews to their hearts so tied
　That they can only live through her.

7

Men sturdy — of discerning eyes,
  And souls to apprehend the right ;
Not with their little light so wise
  They set themselves against thy light.

Men of small reverence for names,
  Courageous, and of fortitude
To put aside the narrow aims
  Of faction, for the public good.

Men loving justice for the race,
  Not for the great ones, and the few,
Less studious of outward grace
  Than careful to be clean all through.

Men holding state, not self, the first,
  Ready when all the deep is tossed
With storms, and worst is come to worst,
  To save the Ship at any cost.

Men upright, and of steady knees,
  That only to the truth will bow ;
Lord, help us choose such men as these,
  For only such can save us now.

ABRAHAM LINCOLN.

FOULLY ASSASSINATED, APRIL 14, 1865. — INSCRIBED TO PUNCH.

No glittering chaplet brought from other lands !
  As in his life, this man, in death, is ours ;
His own loved prairies o'er his " gaunt gnarled hands "
  Have fitly drawn their sheet of summer flowers !

What need hath he now of a tardy crown,
 His name from mocking jest and sneer to save?
When every ploughman turns his furrow down
 As soft as though it fell upon his grave.

He was a man whose like the world again
 Shall never see, to vex with blame or praise;
The landmarks that attest his bright, brief reign
 Are battles, not the pomps of gala-days!

The grandest leader of the grandest war
 That ever time in history gave a place;
What were the tinsel flattery of a star
 To such a breast! or what a ribbon's grace!

'Tis to th' *man*, and th' man's honest worth,
 The nation's loyalty in tears upsprings;
Through him the soil of labor shines henceforth
 High o'er the silken broideries of kings.

The mechanism of external forms —
 The shrifts that courtiers put their bodies through,
Were alien ways to him — his brawny arms
 Had other work than posturing to do!

Born of the people, well he knew to grasp
 The wants and wishes of the weak and small;
Therefore we hold him with no shadowy clasp —
 Therefore his name is household to us all.

Therefore we love him with a love apart
 From any fawning love of pedigree —
His was the royal soul and mind and heart —
 Not the poor outward shows of royalty.

Forgive us then, O friends, if we are slow
    To meet your recognition of his worth —
We're jealous of the very tears that flow
    From eyes that never loved a humble hearth.

SAVED.

No tears for him! his light was not *your* light ;
    From earth to heaven his spirit went and came,
Seeing, where ye but saw the blank, black night,
    The golden breaking of the day of fame.

Faded by the diviner life, and worn,
    Dust has returned to dust, and what ye see
Is but the ruined house wherein were borne
    The birth-pangs of his immortality.

Hither and thither drifting drearily,
    The glory of serener worlds he won,
As some strange shifting column of the sea
    Catches the steadfast splendor of the sun.

What was your shallow love? or what the gleam
    Of smiles that chance and accident could chill,
To him whose soul could make its mate a dream,
    And wander through the universe at will?

When your weak hearts to stormy passion woke,
    His from its loftier bent was only stirred,
As is the broad green bosom of the oak
    By the light flutter of the summer bird.

His joys, in realms forbidden to you, he sought,
  And bodiless servitors, at his commands,
Hovered about the watchfires of his thought
  On the dim borders of poetic lands.

The times he lived in, like a hard, dark wall,
  He grandly painted with his woes and wrongs —
Come nearer, friends, and see how brightly all
  Is joined with silvery mortises of songs.

Weep for yourselves bereft, but not for him ;
  Wrong reaches to the compensating right,
And clouds that make the day of genius dim,
  Shine at the sunset with eternal light.

LOVE POEMS.

SNOWED UNDER.

COME let us talk together,
　　While the sunset fades and dies,
And, darling, look into my heart,
　　And not into my eyes.

Let us sit and talk together
　　In the old, familiar place,
But look deep down into my heart,
　　Not up into my face.

And with tender pity shield me —
　　I am just a withered bough —
I was used to have your praises,
　　And you cannot praise me now.

You would nip the blushing roses ;
　　They were blighted long ago,
But the precious roots, my darling,
　　Are alive beneath the snow.

And in the coming spring-time
　　They will all to beauty start —
Oh, look not in my face, beloved,
　　But only in my heart !

You will not find the little buds,
　　So tender and so bright;
They are snowed so deeply under,
　　They will never come to light.

So look, I pray you, in my heart,
　　And not into my face,
And think about that coming Spring
　　Of greenness and of grace,

When from the winter-laden bough
　　The weight of snow shall drop away,
And give it strength to spring into
　　The life of endless May

AN EMBLEM.

WHAT is my little sweetheart like, d'you say?
　　A simple question, yet a hard, to answer;
But I will tell you in my stammering way
　　The best I can, sir.

When I was young — that's neither here nor there —
　　I read, and reading made my eyelids glisten;
But I'll repeat the story, if you care
　　To stay and listen.

A wild rose, born within a modest glen,
　　And sheltered by the leaves of thorny bushes,
Drooped, being commended to the eyes of men,
　　And died of blushes.

Now, if there were — and one may well suppose
    There never was a flower of such rare splendor,
Much less a rudely nurtured wilding rose,
    Withal so tender —

But say there were ; what is a rose the less,
    When all from east to west the May is blazing,
That any tuneful bard her face should miss,
    And give her praising ?

Yet say there did, and that her heart did break,
    As tells the romance of my early reading,
Then I that fair, fond flower for emblem take —
    Sir, are you heeding ? —

Aye, say there were, and that she spent her days
    In ignorance of her proud poetic glory ;
Only her soft death making to the praise
    Of her brief story :

Even such a wild, bright flower, and so apart
    In her low modest house, my little maid is —
Sweet-hearted, shy, and strange to all the art
    Of your fine ladies.

So tender, that to death she needs must grieve,
    Stabbed by the glances of bold eyes, is certain ;
Take you the emblem, then, and give me leave
    To drop the curtain.

QUEEN OF ROSES.

My little love hath made
A garden that all sweetest sweetness holds,
   And there for hours upon a piece of shade
Fringed round with marjoram and marigolds,
     She lieth dreaming, on her arm of pearl,
     My pretty little love — my garden-girl.

The walks are one and all
Enriched along their borders with wild mint,
   And pinks, and gilliflowers, both large and small ;
But where her little feet do leave a print,
     Whether on grass or ground, it doth displace
     And make of non-effect all other grace.

Her speech is all so fair
The winds disgraced, do from her presence run,
   And when she combeth loose her heavenly hair
She giveth entertainment to the sun.
     Oh, just to touch the least of all thy curls,
     My golden head — my queen of garden-girls.

Her shawl-corners of snow
Like wings drop down about her when she stands
   And never queen's lace made so fair a show
As that doth, knitted in her two white hands ;
     The while some sudden look of cold surprise
     Shoots like an angry comet to her eyes.

When she doth walk abroad
Her subject flowers do one and all arise ;

The low ones housèd meekly in the sod
Do kiss her feet — the lofty ones, her eyes.
Oh sad for him whose seeing hath not seen
My rose of roses, and my heart's dear queen.

I'm tying all my hours
With sighs together — " Welladay ! ah me ! "
Because I cannot choose nor words, nor flowers,
Wherewith to lure my Love to marry me !
I'll ask her what the wretched man must say
Who loves a saint, and woo her just that way.

Else in some honeyed phrase
I'll fit a barb no clearest sight can see,
And toss it up and down all cunning ways,
Until I catch and drag her heart to me !
Ah, then I'll tease her, for my life of pain,
For she shall never have it back again.

NOW AND THEN.

" SING me a song, my nightingale,
Hid in among the twilight flowers ;
And make it low," he said, " I pray,
And make it sweet."   But she said, " Nay ;
Come when the morn begins to trail
Her golden glories o'er the gray —
Morn is the time for love's all-hail ! "
He said, " The morning is not ours !

" Then give me back, my heart's delight,
Hid in among the twilight flowers,

The kiss I gave you yesterday —
　　See how the moon this way has leant,
　　As if to yield a soft consent.
･ Surely," he said, " you will requite
My love in this ? "　　But she said, " Nay."
" Yea, now," he said.　But she said, " Hush !
And come to me at morning-blush."
　　He said, " The morning is not ours !

" But say, at least, you love me, Love.
　　Hid in among the twilight flowers ;
No winds are listening, far or near —
The sleepy doves will never hear."
" Ah, leave me in my sacred glen ;
　　And when the saffron morn shall close
　　Her misty arms about the rose,
Come, and my speech, my thought shall prove —
Not now," she said ; " not now, but then."
　　He said, " The morning is not ours ! "

THE LADY TO THE LOVER.

Since thou wouldst have me show
　In what sweet way our love appears to me,
　Think of sweet ways, the sweetest that can be,
And thou may'st partly dream, but can'st not know ;
　　For out of heaven no bliss —
　　Disshadowed lies, like this,
Therefore similitudes thou must forego.

Thou seem'st myself's lost part,
  That hath, in a new compact, dearer close;
  And if that thou shouldst take a broken rose
And fit the leaves again about the heart,
    That mended flower would be
    A poor, faint sign to thee '
Of how one's self about the other grows.

Think of the sun and dew
  Walled in some little house of leaves from sight,
  Each from the other taking, giving light,
And interpenetrated through and through;
    Feeding, and fed upon —
    All given, and nothing gone,
And thou art still as far as day from night.

Sweeter than honey-comb
  To little hungry bees, when rude winds blow;
  Brighter than wayside window-lights that glow
Through the cold rain, to one that has no home;
    But out of heaven, no bliss
    Disshadowed lies, like this, —
Therefore similitudes thou must forego.

LOVE'S SECRET SPRINGS.

In asking how I came to choose
  This flower that makes my brow to shine,
  You seem to say, you did not lose
    Your choice, my friend, when I had mine!
  And by your lifted brow, exclaim,
" What charms have charmed you? name their name!"

Nay, pardon me — I cannot say
   These are the charms, and those the powers,
And being in a trance one day,
   I took her for my flower of flowers.
Love doth not flatter what he gives —
But here, sir, are some negatives.

'Tis not the little milk-white hands
   That grace whatever work they do ;
'Tis not the braided silken bands
   That shade the eyes of tender blue ;
And not the voice so low and sweet
That holds me captive at her feet.

'Tis not in frowns, knit up with smiles,
   Wherewith she scolds me for my sins,
Nor yet in tricksy ways nor wiles
   That I can say true love begins !
Out of such soil it did not grow ;
It was, — and that is all I know.

'Tis not her twinkling feet so small,
   Nor shoulder glaucing from her sleeve,
Nor yet her virtues, one nor all —
   Love were not love to ask our leave .
She was not wooed, nor was I won —
What draws the dew-drop to the sun ?

Pardon me, then, I cannot tell, —
   Nor can you hope to understand, —
Why I should love my love so well ;
   Nor how, upon this border land,
It fell that she should go with me
Through time into eternity.

AT SEA.

BROWN-FACED sailor, tell me true —
    Our ship I fear is but illy thriving,
Some clouds are black and some are blue,
The women are huddled together below,
Above the captain treads to and fro ;
Tell me, for who shall tell but you,
    Whither away our ship is driving !

The wind is blowing a storm this way,
    The bubbles in my face are winking —
'Tis growing dark in the middle of day,
And I cannot see the good green land,
Nor a ridge of rock, nor a belt of sand ;
Oh, kind sailor, speak and say,
    How long might a little boat be sinking ?

More saucily the bubbles wink ;
    God's mercy keep us from foul weather,
And from drought with nothing but brine to drink.
I dreamed of a ship with her ribs stove in,
Last night, and waking thought of my sin ;
How long would a strong man swim, d'y' think,
    If we were all in th' sea together ?

The sailor frowned a bitter frown,
    And answered, " Aye, there will be foul weather, —
All men must die, and some must drown,
And there isn't water enough in the sea
To cleanse a sinner like you or me ;
O Lord, the ships I've seen go down,
    Crew and captain and all together ! "

The sailor smiled a smile of cheer,
  And looked at me a look of wonder,
And said, as he wiped away a tear,
" Forty years I've been off the land
And God has held me safe in his hand:
He ruleth the storm — He is with us here,
  And his love for us no sin can sunder."

A CONFESSION.

I KNOW a little damsel
  As light of foot as the air,
And with smile as gay
As th' sun o' th' May
  And clouds of golden hair.
She sings with the larks at morning,
  And sings with the doves at e'en,
And her cheeks they shine
Like a rose on the vine,
  And her name is Charlamine.
To plague me and to please me
  She knows a thousand arts,
And against my will
I love her still
  With all my heart of hearts !

I know another damsel
  With eyelids lowly weighed,
And so pale is she
That she seems to me
  Like a blossom blown in the shade.

Her hands are white as charity,
  And her voice is low and sweet,
And she runneth quick
To the sinful and sick,
  And her name is Marguerite.
The broken and bowed in spirit
  She maketh straight and whole,
And I sit at her knee
And she sings to me,
  And I love her with my soul.

I know a lofty lady,
  And her name is Heleanore.
And th' King o' the Sky
In her lap doth lie
  When she sitteth at her door.
Her shoulder is curved like an eagle's wing
  When he riseth on his way,
And my two little maids
They lay in braids
  Her dark locks day by day.
Her heart in the folds of her kerchief,
  It doth not fall or rise,
And afar I wait
At her royal gate,
  And I love her with my eyes !

Now you that are wise in love-lore,
  Come teach your arts to me,
For each of the darling damsels
  Is as sweet as she can be !
And if I wed with Charlamine
  Of the airy little feet,

I shall sicken and sigh,
I shall droop and die,
   For my gentle Marguerite!
And if I wed with Marguerite,
   Whom I so much adore,
I shall long to go
From her hand of snow
   To my Lady Heleanore!
And if I wed with Heleanore,
   Whom with my eyes I love,
'Gainst all that is right,
In my own despite,
   I shall false and faithless prove.

EASTER BRIDAL SONG.

HASTE, little fingers, haste, haste!
   Haste, little fingers, pearly;
And all along the slender waist,
   And up and down the silken sleeves
   Knot the darling and dainty leaves,
And wind o' the South, blow light and fast,
   And bring the flowers so early!

Low, droop low, my tender eyes,
   Low, and all demurely,
And make the shining seams to run
Like little streaks o' th' morning sun
   Through silver clouds so purely;
And fall, sweet rain, fall out o' th' skies,
   And bring the flowers so early!

8

Push, little hands, from the bended face
  The tresses crumpled curly,
And stitch the hem in the frill of snow
And give to the veil its misty flow,
  And melt, ye frosts, so surly ;
And shine out, Spring, with your days of grace,
  And bring the flowers so early !

PRODIGAL'S PLEA.

SHINE down, little head, so fair,
  From thy window in the wall ;
Oh, my slighted golden hair,
  Like the sunshine round me fall —
Little head, so fair, so bright,
Fill my darkness with thy light !

Reach me down thy helping hand,
  Little sweetheart, good and true ;
Shamed, and self-condemned, I stand,
  And wilt thou condemn me too ?
Soilure of sin, be sure
Cannot harm thy hand so pure.

With thy quiet, calm my cry
  Pleading to thee from afar.
Is it not enough that I
  With myself should be at war ?
With thy cleanness, cleanse my blood ;
With thy goodness, make me good.

Eyes that loved me once, I pray,
   Be not crueller than death ;
Hide each sharp-edged glance away
   Underneath its tender sheath !
Make me not, sweet eyes, with scorn
Mourn that ever I was born !

Oh, my roses ! are ye dead ;
   That in love's delicious day,
Used to flower out ripe and red,
   Fast as kisses plucked away ?
Turn thy pale cheek, little wife ;
Let me warm them back to life.

I have wandered, oh, so far !
   From the way of truth and right ;
Shine out for my guiding star,
   Little head, so dear and bright ;
Dust of sin is on my brow—
Good enough for both, art thou !

THE SEAL-FISHER'S WIFE.

THE west shines out through lines of jet,
Like the side of a fish through the fisher's net,
   Silver and golden-brown ;
And rocking the cradle, she sings so low,
As backward and forward, and to and fro,
   She cards the wool for her gown.

She sings her sweetest, she sings her best,
And all the silver fades in the west,

And all the golden-brown,
And lowly leaning cradle across,
She mends the fire with faggots and moss,
    And cards the wool for her gown.

Gray and cold, and cold and gray,
Over the look-out and over the bay,
    The sleet comes sliding down,
And the blaze of the faggots flickers thin,
And the wind is beating the ice-blocks in,
    As she cards the wool for her gown.

The fisher's boats in the ice are crushed.
And now her lullaby-song is hushed, —
    For sighs the singing drown, —
And all, with fingers stiff and cold,
She covers the cradle, fold on fold,
    With the carded wool of her gown.

And there — the cards upon her knee,
And her eyes wide open toward the sea,
    Where the fisher's boats went down —
They found her all as cold as sleet,
And her baby smiling up so sweet,
    From the carded wool of her gown.

CARMIA.

MY Carmia, my life, my saint,
No flower is sweet enough to paint
    Thy sweet, sweet face for me !
The rose-leaf nails, the slender wrist,

The hand, the whitest ever kissed —
Dear Carmia, what has Raphael missed
   In never seeing thee !

Oh to be back among the days
Wherein she blessed me with her praise —
   She knew not how to frown !
The memory of that time doth seem
Like dreaming of a lovely dream,
Or like a golden broider-seam
   Stitched in some homely gown.

No silken skein is half so soft
As those long locks I combed so oft —
   No tender tearful skies —
No violet darkling into jet —
And all with daybreak dew-drops wet —
No star, when first the sun is set,
   Is like my Carmia's eyes.

But not the dainty little wrist,.
Nor hand, the whitest ever kissed,
   Nor face, so sweet to see,
Nor words of praise, that so did bless,
Nor rose-leaf nail, nor silken tress,
   Made her so dear to me.

'Twas nothing my poor words can tell,
Nor charm of chance, nor magic spell
   To wane, and waste, and fall —
I loved her to the utmost strain
Of heart and soul and mind and brain,
And Carmia loved me back again.
   And that is all-and-all !

EPITHALAMIUM.

In the pleasant spring-time weather —
  Rosy morns and purple eves —
When the little birds together
  Sit and sing among the leaves,
Then it seems as if the shadows,
  With their interlacing boughs,
Had been hung above the meadows
  For the plighting of their vows !

In the lighter, warmer weather,
  When the music softly rests,
And they go to work together
  For the building of their nests ;
Then the branches, for a wonder,
  Seem uplifted everywhere,
To be props and pillars under
  Little houses in the air.

But when we see the meeting
  Of the lives that are to run
Henceforward to the beating
  Of two hearts that are as one,
When we hear the holy taking
  Of the vows that cannot break,
Then it seems as if the making
  Of the world was for their sake.

JENNIE.

Now tell me all my fate, Jennie, —
   Why need I plainer speak?
For you see my foolish heart has bled
   Its secret in my cheek!

You must not leave me thus, Jennie, —
   You will not, when you know,
It is my life you're treading on
   At every step you go.

Ah, should you smile as now, Jennie,
   When the wintry weather blows,
The daisy, waking out of sleep,
   Would come up through the snows.

Shall our house be on the hill, Jennie,
   Where the sumach hedges grow?
You must kiss me, darling, if it's yes,
   And kiss me if it's no.

It shall be very fine — the door
   With bean-vines overrun,
And th' window toward the harvest-field
   Where first our love begun.

What marvel that I could not mow
   When you came to rake the hay,
For I cannot speak your name, Jennie,
   If I've nothing else to say.

Nor is it strange that when I saw
　　Your sweet face in a frown,
I hung my scythe in the apple-tree,
　　And thought the sun was down.

For when you sung the tune that ends
　　With such a golden ring
The lark was made ashamed, and sat
　　With her head beneath her wing.

You need not try to speak, Jennie,
　　You blush and tremble so,
But kiss me, darling, if it's yes,
　　And kiss me if it's no!

MIRIAM.

LIKE to that little homely flower
　　That never from her rough house stirs
While summer lasts, but sits and combs
　　The sunbeams with her purple burs,

So kept she in her house content
　　While love's bright summer with her stayed;
But change works change, and since she met
　　A shadow from the land of shade;

The ghost of that wild flower that sits
　　In her rough house, and never stirs
While summer lasts, has not a face
　　· So dead of meaning, as is hers.

In vain the pitying year puts on
　Her rose-red mornings, for like streams
Lost from the sunlight under banks
　Of wintry darkness, are her dreams.

In vain among their clouds of green
　The wild birds sing — she says with tears
Their sweet tongues stammer in the tunes
　They sang so well in other years.

Her home in ruins lies, and thorns
　Choke with their briery arms, the door ;
What matter, says she, since that love
　Will cross the threshold, never more.

POEMS OF NATURE AND HOME.

GOING TO COURT.

THE farm-lad quarried from the mow
   The golden bundles, hastily,
And, giving oxen, colt, and cow
   Their separate portions, he was free.

Then, emptying all the sweet delight
   Of his young heart into his eyes,
As if he might not go that night,
   He lingered, looking at the skies.

The evening's silver plough had gone
   Through twilight's bank of yellow haze,
And turned two little stars thereon —
   Still artfully he stayed to praise

The hedge-row's bloom — the trickling run —
   The crooked lane, and valley low —
Each pleasant walk, indeed, save one,
   And that the way he meant to go !

In truth, for Nature's simple shows
   He had no thoughts that night, to spare,
In vain to please his eyes, the rose
   Climbed redly out upon the air.

The bean-flower, in her white attire
  Displayed in vain her modest charms,
And apple-blossoms, all on fire,
  Fell uninvited in his arms.

When Annie raked the summer hay
  Last year, a little thorn he drew
Out of her white hand, such a way,
  It pierced his heart all through and through

Poor farmer-lad! could he that night
  Have seen how fortune's leaves were writ,
His eyes had emptied all their light
  Back to his heart, and broken it.

ON THE SEA.

I WILL call her when she comes to me
  My lily, and not my wife,
So whitely and so tenderly
  She was set in my stormy life.

In vain her gentle eyes to please
  The year had done her best,
Setting her tides of crocuses
  All softly toward the west:

The bright west, where our love was born
  And grew to perfect bloom,
And where the broad leaves of the corn
  Hang low about her tomb.

I hid from men my cruel wound
  And sailed away on the sea,
But like waves around some hulk aground
  Her love enfoldeth me.

My clumsy hands are cracked and brown ;
  My chin is rough as a bur,
But under the dry husk soft as down
  Lieth my love for her.

One night when storms were in the sky —
  Sailing away on the sea,
I dreamed that I was doomed to die,
  And that she came to me.

They bound my eyes, but I had sight
  And saw her take that hour
My head so bright in her apron white
  As if it had been a flower !

No child when I sit alone at night
  Comes climbing on my knee,
But I dream of love and my heart is light
  As I sail away on the sea.

A FRAGMENT.

IT was a sandy level wherein stood
  The old and lonesome house ; far as the eye
Could measure, on the green back of the wood,
  The smoke lay always, low and lazily.

Down the high gable windows, all one way,
  Hung the long, drowsy curtains, and across
The sunken shingles, where the rain would stay,
  The roof was ridged, a hand's breadth deep, with moss.

The place was all so still you would have said
  The picture of the Summer, drawn, should be
With golden ears, laid back against her head,
  And listening to the far, low-lying sea.

But from the rock, rough-grained and icy-crowned,
  Some little flower from out some cleft will rise ;
And in this quiet land my love I found,
  With all their soft light, sleepy, in her eyes.

No bush to lure a bird to sing to her —
  In depths of calm the gnats' faint hum was drowned,
And the wind's voice was like a little stir
  Of the uneasy silence, not like sound.

No tender trembles of the dew at close
  Of day, — at morn, no insect choir ;
No sweet bees at sweet work about the rose,
  Like little housewife fairies round their fire.

And yet the place, suffused with her, seemed fair —
  Ah, I would be immortal, could I write
How from her forehead fell the shining hair,
  As morning falls from heaven — so bright ! so bright

SHADOWS.

WHEN I see the long wild briers
Waving in the winds like fires,
   See the green skirts of the maples
Barred with scarlet and with gold,
See the sunflower, heavy-hearted,
Shadows then from days departed
   Come and with their tender trembles
Wrap my bosom, fold on fold.

I can hear sweet invitations
Through the sobbing, sad vibrations
   Of the winds that follow, follow,
As from self I seek to fly —
Come up hither ! come up hither !
Leave the rough and rainy weather !
   Come up where the royal roses
Never fade and never die !

'Twas when May was blushing, blooming,
Brown bee, bluebirds, singing, humming,
   That we built and walled our chamber
With the emerald of leaves ;
Made our bed of yellow mosses,
Soft as pile of silken flosses,
   Dreamed our dreams in dewy brightness
Radiant like the morns and eves.

And it was when woods were gleaming,
And when clouds were wildly streaming
   Gray and umber white and ember,

Streaming in the north wind's breath,
That my little rose-mouthed blossom
Fell and faded on my bosom,
   Cankered by the coming coldness,
Blighted by the frosts of death.

Therefore, when I see the shadows,
Drifting in across the meadows,
   See the troops of Summer wild birds
Flying from us, cloud on cloud,
Memory with that May-time lingers,
And I seem to feel the fingers
   Of my lost and lovely darling
Wrap my heart up in her shroud.

APRIL.

THE wild and windy March once more
   Has shut his gates of sleet,
And given us back the April-time,
   So fickle and so sweet.

Now blighting with our fears, our hopes —
   Now kindling hopes with fears —
Now softly weeping through her smiles —
   Now smiling through her tears.

Ah, month that comes with rainbows crowned,
   And golden shadows dressed —
Constant to her inconstancy,
   And faithful to unrest.

The swallows 'round the homestead eaves —
　The bluebirds in the bowers
Twitter their sweet songs for thy sake,
　Gay mother of the flowers.

The brooks that moaned but yesterday
　Through bunches of dead grass,
Climb up their banks with dimpled hands,
　And watch to see thee pass.

The willow, for thy grace's sake,
　Has dressed with tender spray,
And all the rivers send their mists
　To meet thee on the way.

The morning sets her rosy clouds
　Like hedges in the sky,
And o'er and o'er their dear old tunes
　The winds of evening try.

Before another week has gone,
　Each bush, and shrub, and tree,
Will be as full of buds and leaves
　As ever it can be.

I welcome thee with all my heart,
　Glad herald of the Spring,
And yet I cannot choose but think
　Of all thou dost not bring.

The violet opes her eyes beneath
　The dew-fall and the rain —

But oh, the tender, drooping lids
　That open not again !

Thou set'sts the red, familiar rose
　Beside the household door,
But oh, the friends, the sweet, sweet friends
　Thou bringest back no more !

But shall I mourn that thou no more
　A short-lived joy can bring,
Since death has lifted up the gates
　Of their eternal Spring ?

POPPIES.

O LADIES, softly fair,
　Who curl and comb your hair,
And deck your dainty bodies, eve and morn,
　With pearls, and flowery spray,
　And knots of ribbons gay,
As if ye were for idlesse only born :
　Hearken to Wisdom's call —
　What are ye, after all,
But foolish poppies in among the corn !

　Whose lives but parts repeat —
　Whose little dancing feet
Swim lightly as the silverly mists of morn :
　Whose pretty palms unclose
　Like some fresh dewy rose,

For dainty dalliance, not for distaffs born ;
  Hearken to Wisdom's call —
  What are ye, after all,
But flaunting poppies in among the corn !

    O Women, sad of face,
    Whose crowns of girlish grace
Sin has plucked off, and left ye all forlorn —
    Whose pleasures do not please —
    Whose hearts have no hearts'-ease —
Whose seeming honor is of honor shorn :
    Hearken to Wisdom's call —
    What are ye, one and all,
But painted poppies in among the corn !

    Women, to name whose name
    All good men blush for shame,
And bad men even, with the speech of scorn ;
    Who have nor sacred sight
    For Vesta's lamps so white,
Nor hearing for old Triton's wreathèd horn :
    Oh, hark to Wisdom's call —
    What are ye, one and all,
But poison poppies in among the corn !

    Women, who will not cease
    From toil, nor be at peace
Either at purple eve or yellowing morn,
    But drive with pitiless hand,
    Your ploughshares through the land
Quick with the lives of daisies yet unborn :
    Hearken to Wisdom's call —
    What are ye, after all,
But troublous poppies in among the corn !

Blighting with fretful looks
The tender-tasseled stocks —
Sweeping your wide-floored barns with sighs forlorn
About the unfilled grains
And starving hunger-pains
That on the morrow, haply, shall be borne:
Oh, hark to Wisdom's call —
What are ye, after all,
But forward poppies in among the corn!

O Virgins, whose pure eyes
Hold commerce with the skies —
Whose lives lament that ever ye were born;
The cross whose joy to wear
Never the rose, but only just the thorn:
Hearken to Wisdom's call —
What are ye, after all,
Better than poppies in among the corn!

What better? who abuse
The gifts wise women use,
With locks sheared off, and bosoms scourged and torn;
Lapping your veils so white
Betwixt ye and the light
Composed in heaven's sweet cisterns, morn by morn:
Oh, hark to Wisdom's call —
What are ye, after all
Better than poppies in among the corn!

O Women, rare and fine,
Whose mouths are red with wine
Of kisses of your children, night and morn,
Whose ways are virtue's ways —
Whose good works are your praise —

Whose hearts hold nothing God has made in scorn :
 Though Fame may never call
 Your names, ye are, for all,
The Ruths that stand breast-high amid the corn !

 Your steadfast love and sure
 Makes all beside it poor ;
Your cares like royal ornaments are worn ;
 Wise Women ! what so sweet,
 So queenly, so complete
To name ye by, since ever one was born ?
 Since she, whom poets call,
 The sweetest of you all,
First gleaned with Boaz in among the corn.

_ A SEA SONG.

NOR far nor near grew shrub nor tree,
The bare hills stood up bleak behind,
And in between the marsh weeds gray
Some tawny-colored sand-drift lay,
Opening a pathway to the sea,
The which I took to please my mind.

In full sight of the open seas
A patch of flowers I chance to find,
As if the May, being thereabout,
Had from her apron spilled them out ;
And there I lay and took my ease,
And made a song to please my mind.

Sweet bed! if you should live full long,
A sweeter you will never find —
Some flowers were red, and some were white;
And in their low and tender light
I meditated on my song,
Fitting the words to please my mind.

Some sea-waves on the sands upthrown,
And left there by the wanton wind,
With lips all curled in homesick pain
For the old mother's arms again,
Moved me, and to their piteous moan
I set the tune to please my mind.

But now I would in very truth
The flowers I had not chanced to find,
Nor lain their speckled leaves along,
Nor set to that sad tune my song;
For that which pleased my careless youth
It faileth now to please my mind.

And this thing I do know for true,
A truer you will never find,
No false step e'er so lightly rung
But that some echo giving tongue
Did like a hound all steps pursue,
Until the world was left behind.

FORGIVENESS.

Oᴴ, thou who dost the sinner meet,
  Fearing his garment's hem,

Think of the Master, and repeat,
" Neither do I condemn ! "
And while the eager rabble stay,
    Their storms of wrath to pour,
Think of the Master still, and say,
" Go thou, and sin no more ! "

WINTER AND SUMMER.

THE Winter goes and the Summer comes,
    And the cloud descends in warm, wet showers ;
The grass grows green where the frost has been,
    And waste and wayside are fringed with flowers.

The Winter goes and the Summer comes,
    And the merry bluebirds twitter and trill,
And the swallow swings on his steel-blue wings,
    This way and that way, at wildest will.

The Winter goes and the Summer comes,
    And the swallow he swingeth no more aloft,
And the bluebird's breast swells out of her nest,
    And the horniest bill of them all grows soft.

The Summer goes and the Winter comes,
    And the daisy dies and the daffodil dies,
And the softest bill grows horny and still,
    And the days set dimly and dimly rise.

The Summer goes and the Winter comes
    And the red fire fades from the heart o' th' rose,

And the snow lies white where the grass was bright,
  And the wild wind bitterly blows and blows.

The Winter comes and the Winter stays,
  Aye, cold and long and long and cold,
And the pulses beat to the weary feet,
  And the head feels sick and the heart grows cold.

The Winter comes and the Winter stays,
  And all the glory behind us lies,
The cheery light drops into the night,
  And the snow drifts over our sightless eyes.

AUTUMN.

SHORTER and shorter now the twilight clips
  The days, as through the sunset gates they crowd,
And Summer from her golden collar slips
  And strays through stubble-fields, and moans aloud,

Save when by fits the warmer air deceives,
  And, stealing hopeful to some sheltered bower,
She lies on pillows of the yellow leaves,
  And tries the old tunes over for an hour.

The wind, whose tender whisper in the May
  Set all the young blooms listening through th' grove,
Sits rustling in the faded boughs to-day
  And makes his cold and unsuccessful love.

The rose has taken off her tire of red —
  The mullein-stalk its yellow stars have lost,

And the proud meadow-pink hangs down her head
  Against earth's chilly bosom, witched with frost.

The robin, that was busy all the June,
  Before the sun had kissed the topmost bough,
Catching our hearts up in his golden tune,
  Has given place to the brown cricket now.

The very cock crows lonesomely at morn —
  Each flag and fern the shrinking stream divides —
Uneasy cattle low, and lambs forlorn
  Creep to their strawy sheds with nettled sides.

Shut up the door : who loves me must not look
  Upon the withered world, but haste to bring
His lighted candle, and his story-book,
  And live with me the poetry of Spring.

DAMARIS.

You know th' forks of th' road, and th' brown mill?
  And how th' mill-stream, where th' three elms
      grow,
  Flattens its curly head and slips below
That shelf of rocks which juts from out th' hill?

You know th' field of sandstone, red and gray,
  Sloped to th' south? and where th' sign-post stands,
  Silently lifting up its two black hands
To point th' uneasy traveller on his way?

You must remember the long rippling ridge
  Of rye, that cut the level land in two,
  And changed from blue to green, from green to blue,
Summer after summer? And th' one-arched bridge,

Under the which, with joy surpassing words,
  We stole to see beneath the speckled breast
  Of th' wild mother, all the clay-built nest
Set round with shining heads of little birds.

Well, midway 'twixt th' rye-ridge and th' mill,
  In the old house with windows to the morn,
  The village beauty, Damaris, was born —
There lives, in " maiden meditation," still.

Stop you and mark, if you that way should pass,
  The old, familiar quince and apple-trees,
  Chafing against the wall with every breeze,
And at the door the flag-stones, set in grass.

There is the sunflower, with her starry face
  Leaned to her love ; and there, with pride elate,
  The prince's-feather — at th' garden-gate
The green-haired plants, all gracious in their place.

You'll think you have not been an hour away —
  Seeing the stones, th' flowers, the knotty trees,
  And 'twixt the palings, strings of yellow bees,
Shining like streaks of light — but, welladay !

If Damaris happen at the modest door,
  In gown of silver gray and cap of snow —
  Your May-day sweetheart, forty years ago —
The brief delusion can delude no more.

A LESSON.

WOODLAND, green and gay with dew,
Here, to-day, I pledge anew
All the love I gave to you

When my heart was young and glad.
And in dress of homespun plaid,
Bright as any flower you had,

Through your bushy ways I trod,
•Or, lay hushed upon your sod
With my silence praising God.

Never sighing for the town —•
Never giving back a frown
To the sun that kissed me brown.

When my hopes were of such stuff,
That my days, though crude enough,
Were with golden gladness rough —

Timid creatures of the air —
Little ground-mice, shy and fair —
You were friendly with me there.

Beeches gray, and solemn firs,
Thickets full of bees and burs,
You were then my schoolmasters,

Teaching me as best you could,
How the evil by the good —
Thorns by flowers must be construed.

Rivulets of silvery sound,
Searching close, I always found
Fretting over stony ground.

And in hollows, cold and wet,
Violets purpled into jet
As if ·bad blood had been let ;

While in every sunny place,
Each one wore upon her face
Looks of true and tender grace.

Leaning from the hedge-row wall,
Gave the rose her sweets to all,
Like a royal prodigal.

And the lily, priestly white,
Made a little saintly light
In her chapel out of sight.

Heedless how the spider spun —
Heedless of the brook that run
Boldly winking at the sun.

When the autumn clouds did pack
Hue on hue, unto that black
That's bluish, like a serpent's back,

Emptying all their cisterns out,
While the winds in fear and doubt
Whirled like dervises about,

And the mushroom, brown and dry,
On the meadow's face did lie,
Shrunken like an evil eye —

Shrunken all its fleshy skin,
Like a lid that wrinkles in
Where an eyeball once had been.

How my soul within me cried,
As along the woodland side
All the flowers fell sick and died.

But when Spring returned, she said,
" They were sleeping, and not dead —
Thus must light and darkness wed."

Since that lesson, even death
Lies upon the glass of faith,
Like the dimness of a breath.

KATRINA ON THE PORCH.

A BIT OF TURNER PUT INTO WORDS.

An old, old house by the side of the sea,
    And never a picture poet would paint;
    But I hold the woman above the saint,
And the light of the hearth is more to me
    Than shimmer of air-built castle.

It fits as it grew to the landscape there —
    One hardly feels as he stands aloof
    Where the sandstone ends, and the red slate roof

Juts over the window, low and square,
   That looks on the wild sea-water.

From the top of the hill so green and high
   There slopeth a level of golden moss,
   That bars of scarlet and amber cross,
And rolling out to the further sky
   Is the world of wild sea-water.

Some starved grape-vineyards round about —
   A zigzag road cut deep with ruts —
   A little cluster of fishers' huts,
And the black sand scalloping in and out
   'Twixt th' land and th' wild sea-water.

Gray fragments of some border towers.
   Flat, pellmell on a circling mound,
   With a furrow deeply worn all round
By the feet of children through the flowers,
   And all by the wild sea-water.

And there, from the silvery break o' th' day
   Till the evening purple drops to the land,
   She sits with her cheek like a rose in her hand,
And her sad and wistful eyes one way —
   The way of the wild sea-water.

And there, from night till the yellowing morn
   Falls over the huts and th' scallops of sand —
   A tangle of curls like a torch in her hand —
She sits and maketh her moan so lorn,
   With the moan of the wild sea-water.

Only a study for homely eyes,
　　And never a picture poet would paint ;
　　But I hold the woman above the saint,
And the light of the humblest hearth I prize
　　O'er the luminous air-built castle.

THE WEST COUNTRY. ·

HAVE you been in our wild west country ? then
　　You have often had to pass
Its cabins lying like birds' nests in
　　The wild green prairie grass.

Have you seen the women forget their wheels
　　As they sat at the door to spin —
Have you seen the darning fall away
　　From their fingers worn and thin,

As they asked you news of the villages
　　Where they were used to be,
Gay girls at work in the factories
　　With their lovers gone to sea !

Ah, have you thought of the bravery
　　That no loud praise provokes —
Of the tragedies acted in the lives
　　Of poor, hard-working folks !

Of the little more, and the little more
　　Of hardship which they press
Upon their own tired hands to make
　　The toil for the children less:

And not in vain ; for many a lad
  Born to rough work and ways,
Strips off his ragged coat, and makes
  Men clothe him with their praise.

THE OLD HOMESTEAD.

WHEN skies are growing warm and bright,
  And in the woodland bowers
The Spring-time in her pale, faint robes
  Is calling up the flowers,
When all with naked little feet
  The children in the morn
Go forth, and in the furrows drop
  The seeds of yellow corn ;
What a beautiful embodiment
  Of ease devoid of pride
Is the good old-fashioned homestead,
  With its doors set open wide!

But when the happiest time is come
  That to the year belongs,
When all the vales are filled with gold,
  And all the air with songs ;
When fields of yet unripened grain,   ·
  And yet ungarnered stores
Remind the thrifty husbandman
  Of ampler threshing-floors,
How pleasant, from the din and dust
  Of the thoroughfare aloof,
Stands the old fashioned homestead,
  With steep and mossy roof!

When home the woodsman plods with axe
  Upon his shoulder swung,
And in the knotted apple-tree
  Are scythe and sickle hung ;
When low about her clay-built nest
  The mother swallow trills,
And decorously slow, the cows
  Are wending down the hills ;
What a blessed picture of comfort
  In the evening shadows red,
Is the good old fashioned homestead,
  With its bounteous table spread !

And when the winds moan wildly,
  When the woods are bare and brown,
And when the swallow's clay-built nest
  From the rafter crumbles down ;
When all the untrod garden-paths
  Are heaped with frozen leaves,
And icicles, like silver spikes,
  Are set along the eaves ;
Then when the book from the shelf is brought,
  And the fire-lights shine and play,
In the good old fashioned homestead,
  Is the farmer's holiday !

But whether the brooks be fringed with flowers,
  Or whether the dead leaves fall,
And whether the air be full of songs,
  Or never a song at all,
And whether the vines of the strawberries
  Or frosts through the grasses run,
And whether it rain or whether it shine
  Is all to me as one,

For bright as brightest sunshine
   The light of memory streams
Round the old-fashioned homestead,
   Where I dreamed my dream of dreams !

CONTRADICTION.

I LOVE the deep quiet — all buried in leaves,
   To sit the day long just as idle as air,
Till the spider grows tame at my elbow, and weaves,
   And toadstools come up in a row round my chair.

I love the new furrows — the cones of the pine,
   The grasshopper's chirp, and the hum of the mote ;
And short pasture-grass where the clover-blooms shine
   Like red buttons set on a holiday coat.

Flocks packed in the hollows — the droning of bees,
   The stubble so brittle — the damp and flat fen ;
Old homesteads I love, in their clusters of trees,
   And children and books, but not women nor men.

Yet, strange contradiction ! I live in the sound
   Of a sea-girdled city — 'tis thus that it fell,
And years, oh, how many ! have gone since I bound
   A sheaf for the harvest, or drank at a well.

And if, kindly reader, one moment you wait
   To measure the poor little niche that you fill,
I think you will own it is custom or fate
   That has made you the creature you are, not your
     will.

10

MY DREAM OF DREAMS.

ALONE within my house I sit ;
  The lights are not for me,
The music, nor the mirth ; and yet
  I lack not company.

So gayly go the gay to meet,
  Nor wait my griefs to mend —
My entertainment is more sweet
  Than thine, to-night, my friend.

Whilst thou, one blossom in thy hand,
  Bewail'st my weary hours,
Upon my native hills I stand
  Waist-deep among the flowers.

I envy not a joy of thine ;
  For while I sit apart
Soft Summer, oh, fond friend of mine,
  Is with me in my heart.

Aye, aye, I'm young to-night once more ;
  The years their hold have loosed,
And on the dear old homestead door
  I'm watching, as I used,

The sunset hang its scarlet fringe
  Along the low white clouds,
While, radiant with their tender tinge,
  My visions come in crowds.

The doves fly homeward over me,
  The red rose bravely gleams,
And first and last and midst I see
  The dream of all my dreams.

I need not say what dream it was,
  Nor how in life's lost hours
It made the glory of the grass,
  The splendor of the flowers.

I need not wait to paint its glow
  With rainbow light nor sun;
Who ever loved that did not know
  There is no dream but one?

My frosty locks grow bright and brown;
  My step is light once more;
The world now dropping darkly down
  Comes greenly up before.

Comes greenly up before my eyes,
  With gracious splendor clad,
That world which now behind me lies
  So darkly dim, so sad.

Shot over with the purpling morn,
  I see the long mists roll,
And hear beneath the tasseled corn
  The winds make tender dole.

I hear, and all my pulses rouse
  And give back trembling thrills,
The farm-boy calling with his cows
  The echoes from the hills.

So soft the plashing of the rain
  Upon the peach-tree leaves,
It hardly breaks the silvery skein
  The dark-browed spider weaves.

The grasshopper so faintly cries
  Beneath the dock's round burs
That in the shadow where she lies
  The silence scarcely stirs.

Bright tangles of the wings of birds
  Along the thickets shine,
But oh, how poor are common words
  To tell of bliss divine !

So let thy soft tears cease to fall,
  My friend, nor longer wait ;
I have my recompense for all
  Thou pitiest in my fate,

The joys thou hold'st within thy glance
  Thou canst not make to last ;
Mine are uplifted to romance —
  Immortal, changeless, fast.

When pleasures fly too far aloof,
  Or pain too sorely crowds,
I go and sit beneath my roof
  Of golden morning clouds.

There back to life my dead hope starts,
  And well her pledge redeems,
As close within my heart of hearts
  I hug my dream of dreams.

POEMS OF LOSS.

THE OTHER SIDE.

I DREAMED I had a plot of ground.
 Once on a time, as story saith,
All closèd in and closèd round
 With a great wall, as black as death.

I saw a hundred mornings break,
 So far a little dream may reach;
And, like a blush on some fair cheek,
 The spring-time mantling over each.

Sweet vines o'erhung, like vernal floods,
 The wall, I thought, and though I spied
The glorious promise of the buds,
 They only bloomed the other side.

Tears, torments, darkened all my ground,
 Yet Heaven, by starts, above me gleamed;
I saw, with senses strangely bound,
 And in my dreaming knew I dreamed.

Saying to my heart, these things are signs
 Sent to instruct us that 'tis ours
Duly to dress and keep our vines,
 Waiting in patience for the flowers.

But when the angel, feared by all,
 Across my hearth his shadow spread,
The rose that climbed my garden wall
 Had bloomed, the other side, I said.

A WINTRY WASTE.

The boughs they blow across the pane,
And my heart is stirred with sudden joy,
For I think 'tis the shadow of my boy,
 My long lost boy, come home again
To love, and to live with me;
And I put the work from off my knee,
And open the door with eager haste —
There lieth the cold, wild winter waste,
 And that is all I see!

The boughs they drag against the eaves,
I hear them early, I hear them late,
And I think 'tis the latch of the door-yard gate,
 Or a step on the frozen leaves.
And I say to my heart, he is slow, he is slow,
And I call him loud and I call him low,
And listen, and listen, again and again,
And I see the wild shadows go over the pane.
And the dead leaves, as they fall,
 I hear, and that is all.

But fancy only half deceives —
My joys are counterfeits of joy,
For I know he never will come, my boy;
 And I see through my make-believes,

Only the wintry waste of snow,
Where he lieth so cold, and lieth so low,
   And so far from the light and me:
And boughs go over the window-pane,
And drag on the lonely eaves, in vain, —
   That waste is all I see.

THE SHADOW.

In vain the morning trims her brows,
   A shadow all the sunshine shrouds;
The moon at evening vainly ploughs
   Her golden furrows in the clouds.

In vain the morn her splendor hath;
   The stars, in vain, their gracious cheer
There moves a phantom on my path,
   A shapeless phantom that I fear.

The summer wears a weary smile,
   A weary hum the woodland fills;
The dusty road looks tired the while
   It climbs along the sleepy hills.

Still do I strive to build my song
   Against this grim aggressive gloom;
Oh hope, I say, be strong, be strong!
   Some special, saving grace must come.

I sit and talk of sunnier skies,
   Of flowers with healing in their gleams,
But still the shapeless shadow flies
   Before me to the land of dreams.

O friends of mine, who sit dismayed
    And watch, I cry, with bated breath ;
Yet from their answering shrink afraid,
    Lest that they name the name of Death.

HOW PEACE CAME.

As the still hours towards midnight wore,
    She called to me — her voice was low
    And soft as snow that falls in snow —
She called my name, and nothing more.

Sleeping, I felt the life-blood stir
    With piercing anguish all my heart —
    I felt my dreams like curtains part,
And straightway passed through them to her.

Yet, 'twixt my answer and her call,
    My thoughts had time enough to run
    Through everything that I had done
From my youth upward.   One and all.

The harmful words which I had said —
    The sinful thoughts, the looks untrue,
    Straight into fearful phantoms grew,
And ranged themselves about her bed.

Weeping, I called her names most sweet,
    But still the phantoms, evil-eyed,
    Between us stood, and though I died,
I could not even touch her feet.

My soul within me seemed to groan —
  My cheek was burning up with shame —
  I called each dark deed by its name,
And humbly owned it for my own.

My tongue was loosed — my heart was free —
  I took the little shining head
  Betwixt my palms — the phantoms fled.
And Heaven was moved, and came to me.

BE STILL.

COME, bring me wild pinks from the valleys,
  Ablaze with the fire o' the sun —
No poor little pitiful lilies
  That speak of a life that is done!

And open the windows to lighten
  The wearisome chamber of •pain —
The eyes of my darling will brighten
  To see the green hill-tops again.

Choose tunes with a lullaby flowing,
  And sing through the watches you keep;
Be soft with your coming and going —
  Be soft! she is falling asleep.

Ah, what would my life be without her!
  Pray God that I never may know!
Dear friends, as you gather about her,
  Be low with your weeping — be low.

Be low, oh, be low with your weeping!
  Your sobs would be sorrow to her;
I tremble lest while she is sleeping
  A rose on her pillow should stir.

Sing slower, sing softer and slower!
  Her sweet cheek is losing its red —
Sing low, aye, sing lower and lower —
  Be still, oh, be still! She is dead.

VANISHED.

Out of the wild and weary night
  I see the morning softly rise,
  But oh, my lovely, lovely eyes!
The world is dim without your light.

I see the young buds break and start
  To fresher life when frosts are o'er,
  But oh, my rose-red mouth! no more
Will kiss of yours delight my heart.

The worm that knows nor hope nor trust
  Comes forth with glorious wings dispread,
  But oh, my little golden head!
I see you only in the dust.

I hear the calling of the lark,
  Despite the cloud, despite the rain;
  But oh, my snow-white hands! in vain
I search to find you through the dark.

When the strong whirlwind's rage is o'er,
  A whisper bids the land rejoice;
  But oh, my gentle, gentle voice
Your music gladdens me no more

But though no earthly joy dispel
  This gloom that fills my life with woe,
  My sweetest, and my best! I know
That you are still alive and well.

Alive and well: oh, blissful thought!
  In some sweet clime, I know not where;
  I only know that you are there,
And sickness, pain, and death are not.

SAFE.

AH, she was not an angel to adore,
  She was not perfect — she was only this:
  A woman to be prattled to, to kiss,
To praise with all sweet praises, and before
  Whose face you never were ashamed to lay
  The affections of your pride away.

I have kept Fancy travelling to and fro
  Full many an hour, to find what name were best,
  If there were any sweeter than the rest,
That I might always call my darling so;
  And this of woman seems to me the sweetest,
  The finest, the most gracious, the completest.

The dust she wore about her I agree
  Was poor and sickly, even to make you sad,
  But this rough world we live in never had
An ornament more excellent than she ;
  The earthly dress was all so frail that you
Could see the beauteous spirit shining through.

Not what she was, but what she was to me
  Is what I fain would tell — from her was drawn
  The softness of the eve, the light of dawn ;
With her and for her I could only see
  What things were sweet and sensible and pure ;
Now all is dull, slow guessing, nothing sure.

My sorrow with this comfort yet is stilled —
  I do not dread to hear the Winter stir
  His wild winds up — I have no fear for her :
And all my love could never hope to build
  A place so sweet beneath heaven's arch of blue,
As she by death has been elected to.

WAITING.

Ah yes, I see the sunshine play,
  I hear the robin's cheerful call,
But I am thinking of the day
  My darling left me — that is all.

I do not grieve for her — ah no !
  To her the way is clear, I trust ;
But for myself I grieve, so low,
  So weak, so in, and of the dust.

And for my sadness I am sad —
  I would be gay if so I might,
But she was all the joy I had —
  My life, my love, my heart's delight.

We came together to the door
  Of our sweet home that is to be,
And knowing, she went in before,
  To put on marriage robes for me.

'Tis weary work to wait so long,
  But true love knows not how to doubt;
God's wisdom fashions seeming wrong,
  That we may find right meanings out.

INTIMATIONS.

THERE is hovering about me
  A power so sweet, so sweet,
That I know, despite my sorrow,
  We assuredly shall meet.
I know, and thus the darkness
  In between us, is defied,
That death is but a shadow
With the sunshine either side.

The world is very weary,
  But I never cease to know
That still there is a border-land,
  Where spirits come and go;
For you send me intimations
  In the morning's gentle beams,

And at night you come and meet me
  In the golden gate of dreams.

I am desolate and dreary,
  But mortal pain and doubt
Are blessings, and our part it is
  To find their meanings out:
To find their blessed meanings,
  And to wait in hope and trust,
Till our gracious Lord and Master
  Shall redeem us from the dust.

LAST POEMS OF PHŒBE CARY.

BALLADS.

DOVECOTE MILL.

THE HOMESTEAD.

From the old Squire's dwelling, gloomy and grand,
Stretching away on either hand,
Lie fields of broad and fertile land.

Acres on acres everywhere
The look of smiling plenty wear,
That tells of the master's thoughtful care.

Here blossoms the clover, white and red,
Here the heavy oats in a tangle spread;
And the millet lifts her golden head.

And, ripening, closely neighbored by
Fields of barley and pale white rye,
The yellow wheat grows strong and high

And near, untried through the summer days,
Lifting their spears in the sun's fierce blaze,
Stand the bearded ranks of the maize.

Straying over the side of the hill,
Here the sheep run to and fro at will,
Nibbling of short green grass their fill.

11

Sleek cows down the pasture take their ways,
Or lie in the shade through the sultry days,
Idle, and too full-fed to graze.

Ah, you might wander far and wide,
Nor find a spot in the country side,
So fair to see as our valley's pride !

How, just beyond, if it will not tire
Your feet to climb this green knoll higher.
We can see the pretty village spire ;

And, mystic haunt of the whippoorwills,
The wood, that all the background fills,
Crowning the tops to the mill-creek hills.

There, miles away, like a faint blue line,
Whenever the day is clear and fine
You can see the track of a river shine.

Near it a city hides unseen,
Shut close the verdant hills between,
As an acorn set in its cup of green.

And right beneath, at the foot of the hill,
The little creek flows swift and still,
That turns the wheel of Dovecote Mill.

Nearer the grand old house one sees
Fair rows of thrifty apple-trees,
And tall straight pears, o'ertopping these

And down at the foot of the garden, low,
On a rustic bench, a pretty show,
White bee-hives, standing in a row.

Here trimmed in sprigs with blossoms, each
Of the little bees in easy reach,
Hang the boughs of the plum and peach.

At the garden's head are poplars, tall,
And peacocks, making their harsh loud call,
Sun themselves all day on the wall.

And here you will find on every hand
Walks, and fountains, and statues grand,
And trees from many a foreign land.

And flowers, that only the learned can name,
Here glow and burn like a gorgeous flame,
Putting the poor man's blooms to shame.

Far away from their native air
The Norway pines their green dress wear;
And larches swing their long loose hair.

Near the porch grows the broad catalpa tree
And o'er it the grand wistaria,
Born to the purple of royalty.

There looking the same for a weary while, —
'Twas built in this heavy, gloomy style, —
Stands the mansion, a grand old pile.

Always closed, as it is to-day,
And the proud Squire, so the neighbors say,
Frowns each unwelcome guest away.

Though some who knew him long ago,
If you ask, will shake their heads of snow.
And tell you he was not always so,

Though grave and quiet at any time, —
But that now, his head in manhood's prime,
Is growing white as the Winter's rime.

THE GARDENER'S HOME.

Well, you have seen it — a tempting spot!
Now come with me through the orchard plot
And down the lane to the gardener's cot.

Look where it hides almost unseen,
And peeps the sheltering vines between,
Like a white flower out of a bush of green.

Cosy as nest of a bird inside
Here is no room for show or pride
And the open door swings free and wide.

Across the well-worn stepping stone,
With sweet ground-ivy half o'ergrown,
You may pass, as if the house were your own.

You are welcome here to come or stay,
For to all the host has enough to say;
And the good-wife smiles in a pleasant way.

'Tis a pretty place to see in the time,
When the vines in bloom o'er the rude walls climb,
And Nature laughs in her joyful prime.

Bordered by roses, early and late,
A narrow graveled walk leads straight
Up to the door from the rustic gate.

Here the lilac flings her perfume wide
And the sweet-brier, up to the lattice tied,
Seems trying to push herself inside.

A little off to the right, one sees
Some black and sturdy walnut trees,
And locusts, whose white flowers scent the breeze.

And the Dovecote Mill stands just beyond,
With its dull red walls, and the droning sound
Of the slow wheel, turning round and round.

Here the full creek rushes noisily,
Though oft in Summer it runs half dry,
And its song is only a lullaby.

But the prettiest sight when all is done,
That the eye or mind can rest upon,
Or in the house or out in the sun; —

And whatever beside you may have met,
The picture you will not soon forget, —
Is little Bethy, the gardener's pet.

Ever his honest laughing eyes
Beam with a new and glad surprise,
At the wit of her childish, quaint replies.

While the mother seems with a love more deep
To guard her always, awake or asleep,
As one with a sacred trust to keep.

Here in the square room, parlor and hall,
Stand the stiff-backed chairs against the wall,
And the clock in the corner, straight and tall.

Ranged on the cupboard shelf in sight,
Glistens the china, snowy white,
And the spoons and platters, burnished bright.

Oft will a bird, or a butterfly dare
To venture in through the window, bare,
And opened wide for the summer air.

And sitting near it you may feel
Faint scent of herbs from the garden steal,
And catch the sound of the miller's wheel.

With wife and child, and his plot to till,
Here the gardener lives contented still,
Let the world outside go on as it will.

THE MILL.

With cobwebs and dust on the windows spread,
On the walls and the rafters overhead,
Rises the old mill, rusty red.

Grim as the man who calls it his own
Outside, from the gray foundation stone,
To the roof with spongy moss o'ergrown.

Through a loophole made in the gable high,
In and out like arrows fly
The slender swallows, swift and shy.

And with bosoms purple, brown, and white,
Along the eves, in the shimmering light,
Sits a row of doves from morn till night.

Less quiet far is the place within,
Where the falling meal o'erruns the bin,
And you hear the busy stir and din.

Grave is the miller's mein and pace,
But his boy, with ruddy, laughing face,
Is good to see in this sombre place.

And little Bethy will say to you,
That he is good and brave and true,
And the wisest boy you ever knew!

"Why Robert," she says, "was never heard
To speak a cross or a wicked word,
And he wouldn't injure even a bird!"

And he, with boyish love and pride,
Ever since she could walk by his side,
Has been her playmate and her guide.

For he lived in the world three years before
Bethy her baby beauty wore;
And is taller than she by a head or more.

Up the plank and over the sill,
In and out at their childish will,
They played about the old red mill.

They watched the mice through the corn-sacks steal,
The steady shower of the snowy meal,
And the water falling over the wheel.

They loved to stray in the garden walks,
Bordered by stately hollyhocks
And pinks and odorous marigold stalks.

Where lilies and tulips stood in line
By the candytuft and the columbine,
And lady-grass, like a ribbon fine.

Where the daffodil wore her golden lace,
And the prince's-feather blushed in the face,
And the cockscomb looked as vain as his race.

And here, as gay as the birds in the bowers,
Our children lived through their life's first hours,
And grew till their heads o'ertopped the flowers.

SUGAR-MAKING.

Swiftly onward the seasons flew,
And enough to see and enough to do
Our children found the long year through.

They played in the hay when the fields were mowed,
With the sun-burnt harvesters they rode
Home to the barn a-top of the load.

When her fragrant fruit the orchard shed,
They helped to gather the apples spread
On the soft grass — yellow, russet, and red.

Down hill in winter they used to slide,
And over the frozen mill-creek glide,
Or play by the great bright fire inside

The house; or sit in the chimney nook,
Pleased for the hundredth time to look
Over the self-same picture book.

Castles, and men of snow they made,
And fed with crumbs the robins, that stayed
Near the house — half tame, and half afraid.

So ever the winter-time flew fast,
And after the cold short months were past
Came the sugar-making on at last.

'Twas just ere the old folks used to say,
" Now the oaks are turning gray,
'Tis time for the farmer to plant away ! "

Before the early bluebird was there ;
Or down by the brook the willow fair
Loosed to the winds her yellow hair.

Ah ! then there was life and fun enough,
In making the " spile " and setting the trough,
And all, till the time of the " stirring off."

They followed the sturdy hired man,
With his brawny arms and face of tan,
Who gathered the sap each day as it ran,

And they thought it a very funny sight,
The yoke that he wore, like " Buck and Bright,"
Across his shoulders, broad, upright.

They watched the fires, with awe profound,
Go lapping the great black kettles round,
And out the chimney, with rushing sound.

They loved the noise of the brook, that slid
Swift under its icy, broken lid,
And they knew where that delicate flower was hid,

That first in March her head upheaves ;
And they found the tender " adam-and-eves "
Beneath their bower of glossy leaves.

They gathered spice-wood and ginseng roots,
And the boy could fashion whistles and flutes
Out of the paw-pan and walnut shoots.

So every season its pleasure found ;
Though the children never strayed beyond
The dear old hills that hemmed them round.

THE PLAYMATES.

Behind the cottage the mill-creek flowed,
And before it, white and winding, showed
The narrow track of the winter road.

The creek, when low, showed a sandy floor,
And many a green old sycamore
Threw its shade in summer from shore to shore.

And just a quiet country lane,
Fringed close by fields of grass and grain,
Was the crooked road that crossed the plain.

Out of the fragrant fennel's bed
On its bank, the purple iron-weed spread
Her broad top over the mullein's head.

Off through the straggling town it wound,
Then led you down to beech-wood pond,
And up to the school-house, just beyond.

Not far away was a wood's deep shade
Where, larger grown, the boy and maid,
Searching for flowers and berries, strayed,

And oft they went the field-paths through
Where all the things she liked he knew,
And the very places where they grew.

The hidden nook where Nature set
The wind-flower and the violet,
And the mountain-fringe in hollows wet.

The solomon's-seal, of gold so fine,
And the king-cup, holding its dewy wine
Up to the crownèd dandelion.

He gathered the ripe nuts in the fall,
And berries, that grew by fence and wall
So high, she could not reach them at all.

The fruit of the hawthorn, black and red,
Wild grapes, and the hip that came instead,
Of the sweet wild roses, faded and dead.

Then the curious ways of birds he knew,
And where they lived the season through,
And how they built, and sang, and flew.

Sometimes the boughs he bended down,
And Bethy counted with eyes that shone,
Eggs, white and speckled, blue and brown.

And oft they watched with wondering eye
The swallows, up on the rafters high
Teaching their timid young to fly.

For many a dull and rainy day
They wiled the hours till night away
Up in the mow on the scented hay.

And many a dress was soiled and torn
In climbing about the dusty barn
And up to the lofts of wheat and corn.

For they loved to hear on the roof, the rain,
And to count the bins, again and again,
Heaped with their treasures of golden grain.

They played with the maize's sword-like leaves
And tossed the rye and the oaten sheaves,
In Autumn piled to the very eaves.

They peeped in the stalls where the cattle fed,
They fixed their swing to the beam o'erhead, —
Turned the wind-mill, huge, and round, and red.

And the treasure of treasures, the pet and toy,
The source alike of his care and joy,
Was the timid girl to the brave bright boy.

When they went to school, her hand he took,
Led her, and helped her over stile and brook,
And carried her basket, slate, and book.

And he was a scholar, if Bethy said true,
The hardest book he could read right through,
And there wasn't a " sum " that he couldn't " do ! "

Oh, youth, whatever we lose or secure,
One good we can all keep safe aud sure,
Who remember a childhood, happy and pure !

And hard indeed must a man be made,
By the toil and traffic of gain and trade,
Who loves not the spot where a boy he played.

And I pity that woman, or grave or gay,
Who keeps not fresh in her heart alway
The tender dreams of her life's young day !

THE SCHOOL.

Swiftly the seasons sped away,
And soon to our children came the day
When their life had work as well as play.

When they trudged each morn to the school-house set
Where the winter road and the highway met —
Ah ! how plainly I see it yet !

With its noisy play-ground trampled so
By the quick feet, running to and fro,
That not a blade of grass could grow.

And the maple-grove across the road,
The hollow where the cool spring flowed,
Aud greenly the mint and calamus showed.

And the house — unpainted, dingy, low,
Shielded a little from sun and snow,
By its three stiff locusts, in a row.

I can see the floor, all dusty and bare,
The benches hacked, the drawings rare
On the walls, and the master's desk and chair :

And himself, not withered, cross, and grim,
But a youth, well-favored, shy, and slim ;
More awed by the girls than they by him.

With a poet's eye and a lover's voice,
Unused to the ways of rustic boys
And shrinking from all rude speech and noise.

Where is he?   Where should we find again
The children who played together there ?
If alive, sad women and thoughtful men :

Where now is Eleanor proud and fine ?
And where is dark-eyed Angivine,
Rebecca, Annie, and Caroline ?

And timid Lucy with pale gold hair,
And soft brown eyes that unaware
Drew your heart to her, and held it there ?

There was blushing Rose, the beauty and pride
Of her home, and all the country side ;
She was the first we loved who died.

And the joy and pride of our life's young years,
The one we loved without doubts or fears,
Alas ! to-day he is named with tears.

And Alice, with quiet, thoughtful way
Yet joining always in fun and play,
God knows she is changed enough to-day !

I think of the boy no father claimed,
Of him, a fall from the swing had lamed,
And the girl whose hand in the mill was maimed.

And the lad too sick and sad to play,
Who ceased to come to school one day,
And on the next he had passed away.

And I know the look the master wore
When he told us our mate of the day before
Would never be with us any more !

And how on a grassy slope he was laid —
We could see the place from where we played —
A sight to make young hearts afraid.

Sometimes we went by two and three,
And read on his tombstone thoughtfully,
" As I am now so you must be."

Brothers with brothers fighting, slain,
From out those school-boys some have lain
Their bones to bleach on the battle-plain.

Some have wandered o'er lands and seas,
Some haply sit in families,
With children's children on their knees.

Some may have gone in sin astray,
Many asleep by their kindred lay,
Dust to dust, till the judgment day !

YOUTH AND MAIDEN.

A half score years have sped away
Since Robert and Bethy used to play
About the yard and the mill, all day.

For time must go, whatever we do ;
And the boy as it went, to manhood grew,
Steady and honest, good and true.

Going on with the mill, when his father died ;
He lived untempted there, untried,
Knowing little of life beside.

12

Striving not to be rich or great,
Never questioning fortune or fate,
Contented slowly to earn, and wait.

Doing the work that was near his hand,
Still of Bethy he thought and planned,
To him the flower of all the land.

And tall shy Bethy more quiet seems,
With a tenderer light her soft eye beams,
And her thoughts are vague as the dream of dreams.

Oft she sings in an undertone
Of fears and sorrows not her own, —
The pains that love-lorn maids have known.

Does she think as she breathes the tender sigh,
Of the lover that's coming, by and by ?
If she will not tell you, how should I ?

And when she walks in the evenings bland
Over the rich squire's pleasant land,
Does she long to be a lady, grand,

And to have her fingers, soft and white,
Lie in her lap, with jewels bright,
And with never a task from morn till night ?

Often, walking about the place,
With bended head and thoughtful face,
She meets the owner face to face.

Sometimes he eyes her wistfully,
As blushing with rustic modesty,
She drops him a pretty courtesy,

And looks as if inclined to say
Some friendly word to bid her stay,
Then, silent, turns abrupt away.

And though to speak she never dares,
She is sad to think that no one cares
For the lonely man, with thin gray hairs.

The good-wife, just as the girl was grown,
Went from the places she had known,
And the gardener and Bethy live alone.

THE COUNTRY GRAVE-YARD.

So she goes sometimes past Dovecote Mill,
To the place of humble graves on the hill,
Where the mother rests in the shadows still.

Here, sleeping well as the sons of fame,
Lie youth and maiden, sire and dame,
With never a record but their name.

And some, their very names forgot,
Not even a stone to mark the spot,
Yet sleep in peace ; so it matters not !

Here lieth one, who shouldered his gun,
When the news was brought from Lexington ;
And laid it down, when peace was won.

Still he wore his coat of " army blue,"
Silver buckles on knee and shoe,
And sometimes even his good sword, too.

For however the world might change or gaze,
He kept his ancient dress and ways.
Nor learned the fashion of modern days.

But here he had laid aside his staff,
And you read half-worn, and guessed it half
His quaint and self-made epitaph, —

" Stoop down, my friends, and view his dust
Who turned out one among the first
To secure the rights you hold in trust.

" Support the Constitution, plain !
By being united we form the chain
That binds the tyrant o'er the main ! "

Here from the good dead shut away
By a dismal paling, broken and gray,
Down in the lonesomest corner lay,

A baby, dead in its life's first spring,
And its hapless mother, a fair sad thing,
Who never wore a wedding ring !

Often the maiden's steps are led
Away to a lonely, grassy bed,
With a marble headstone, at its head :

And carved there for memorial,
Half hid by the willow branches' fall,
The one word, " Mercy," that is all.

Whether her life had praise or blame,
All that was told was just the same,
She was a woman, this her name.

What beside there was naught to show,
Though always Bethy longed to know
The story of her who slept below.

What had she been ere she joined the dead ; —
Was she bowed with years, or young instead ;
Was she a maiden, or was she wed ?

Never another footstep here
But the maiden's seemed to come a-near,
Yet flowers were blooming from year to year.

Something, whether of good or harm,
Down to the dead one, like a charm
Drew the living heart, fresh and warm ;

Yet haunts more cheerful our Bethy had,
For youth loves not the things that are sad,
But turns to the hopeful.and the glad.

Though somehow she has grown more shy,
More silent than in days gone by,
Whenever the tall young miller is nigh.

As they walk together, grave and slow,
No longer hand in hand they go :
Who can tell what has changed them so ?

Till the sea shall cease to kiss the shore,
Till men and maidens shall be no more,
'Tis the same old story, o'er and o'er.

Secret hoping, and secret fears,
Blushing and sighing, smiles and tears,
The charm and the glory of life's young years !

WOOING.

Now in the waning autumn days
The dull red sun, with lurid blaze,
Shines through the soft and smoky haze.

Fallen across the garden bed,
Many a flower that reared its head
Proudly in Summer, lies stiff and dead.

The pinks and roses have ceased to blow,
The foxgloves stand in a long black row,
And the daffodils perished long ago.

Now the poplar rears his yellow spire,
The maple lights his fuueral pyre,
And the dog-wood burns like a bush of fire.

The harvest fields are bare again,
The barns are filled to the full with grain
And the orchard trees of their load complaiu.

Huge sacks of corn o'er the floor are strewn,
And Dovecote Mill grinds on and on,
And the miller's work seems never done.

But now 'tis the Sabbath eve, and still
For a little while is the noisy mill
And Robert is free to go where he will.

But think or do whatever he may,
The face of Bethy he sees alway
Just as she looked iu the choir to-day.

And as his thoughts the picture paint,
The hope within his heart grows faint,
As it might before a passionless saint.

Looking away from the book on her knees,
Pretty Bethy at sunset sees,
Some one under the sycamore trees,

Walking and musing slow, apart; —
But why should the blood with sudden start,
Leap to her cheek from her foolish heart?

Oh, if he came now, and if he spake,
What answer should she, could she make?
This was the way her thought would take.

Now, troubled maid on the cottage sill,
Be wise, and keep your pulses still,
He has turned, he is coming up the hill!

How he spake, or she made reply,
How she came on his breast to lie,
She could not tell you, better than I.

But when the stars came out in the skies
He has told his love, in whispered sighs,
And she has answered, with downcast eyes.

For somehow, since the world went round,
For men who are simple, or men profound,
Hath a time and a way to woo been found.

And maids, for a thousand, thousand years,
With trusting hopes, or trembling fears
Have answered blushing through smiles and tears.

And why should these two lovers have more
Of thoughtless folly or wisdom's lore
Than all the world who have lived before?

Nay, she gives her hand to him who won
Her heart, and she says, when this is done,
There is no other under the sun

Could be to her what he hath been;
For he to her girlish fancy then
Was the only man in the world of men.

She is ready to take his hand and name,
For better or worse, for honor or blame; —
God grant it may always be the same.

•

PLIGHTED.

Oh, the tender joy of those autumn hours,
When fancy clothed with spring the bowers,
And the dead leavès under the feet seemed flowers !

Oh, the blessèd, blessèd days of youth,
When the heart is filled with gentle ruth,
And lovers take their dreams for truth.

Oh, the hopes they had, and the plans they planned,
The man and the maid, as hand in hand,
They walked in a fair, enchanted land !

Marred with no jealousy, fear, or doubt,
At worst, but a little pet or pout,
Just for the " making up," no doubt !

Have I said how looked our wood nymph, wild ?
And how in these days she always smiled,
Guileless and glad as a little child ?

Her voice had a tender pleading tone,
She was just a rose-bud, almost grown
Aud before its leaves are fully blown.

Graceful and tall as a lily fair,
The peach lent the bloom to her blushes rare,
And the thrush the brown of her rippling hair

Colored with violet, blue were her eyes,
Stolen from the breeze her gentle sighs,
And her soul was borrowed from the skies.

And you, if a man, could hardly fail,
If you saw her tripping down the dale,
To think her a Princess of fairy tale;

Doomed for a time by charm or spell,
Deep in some lonely, haunted dell,
With mischief-loving elves to dwell.

Or bound for a season, body and soul,
Underneath a great green knoll,
To live alone with a wicked Troll.

You would have feared her form so slight,
Would vanish into the air or light,
Or sudden, sink in the earth from sight.

And you must have looked, and longed to see
The handsome Prince who should set her free
Come riding his good steed gallantly.

Just as fair as the good year's prime,
To our lovers was the cold and rime,
For their bright lives had no winter-time.

The drifts might pile, and the winds might blow,
Still up from the mill to the cottage, low,
There was a straight path cut through the snow.

And it only added another charm
To the cheerful hearth, secure and warm,
To hear on the roof and pane, the storm.

Sometimes Bethy would lightly say,
Partly in earnest, partly in play, —
" I wish it would never again be May ! "

And he would answer, half pleased, half tried,
As he drew her nearer to his side,
Nay, nay, for in Spring I shall have my bride.

And she'd cry in a pretty childish pet,
" Ah ! then you must have whom you can get ;
I shall not marry for ages yet."

Then gravely he'd shake his head at this :
But things went never so far amiss
They were not righted at last by a kiss.

And so the seasons sped merry and fast,
And the budding spring-time came, and passed,
And the wedding day was set at last.

With never a quarrel, scarce a fear,
Each to the other growing more dear,
They kept their wooing a whole sweet year.

WEDDED.

In the village church where a child she was led,
Where a maiden she sang in the choir o'erhead,
There were Bethy and Robert wed.

Strong, yet tender and good looked he,
As he took her almost reverently,
And she was a pleasant sight to see.

And men and women, far and wide,
Came from village and country side
To wish them joy and to greet the bride.

The friends who knew them since they were born,
Each with his best and bravest worn
Did honor to them on their marriage morn

But one at the church was heard to say ·
" The Squire, whom none has seen to-day,
Might have given the bride away,

" Yet his is a face 'twere best to miss ;
And what could he do at a time like this,
But be a cloud on its happiness ?

" So let him stay with his gloom and pride,
For he is not fit to sit beside
The wedding guests, or to kiss the bride."

But Bethy, her heart was soft you know,
To herself, as she heard it, whispered low,
" Who knows what sorrow has made him so ? "

And looking away towards the gloomy hall,
And then at the bridegroom fine and tall,
She said, " I wish he had come, for all ! "

Home through the green and shady lane,
The way their childish feet had ta'en,
They came as man and wife again.

Just to the low old cottage here,
Among the friends and places dear
(For the gardener was not dead a year)

And why, as the great do, should they range?
They needs must find enough of change,
They are come to a world that is new and strange.

Lovingly eventide comes on,
The feast is eaten, the friends are gone,
And wife and husband are left alone.

In kindly parting they have prest
The hand of every lingering guest
And now they shut us out with the rest.

Oh, joy too sacred to look upon,
The very angels may leave alone,
Two happy souls by love made one !

But whatever they gain or whatever they miss
The poor have no time in a world like this,
To waste in sorrow or happiness.

For men who have their bread to earn
Must plant and gather and grind the corn,
And the miller goes to the mill at morn.

He blushes a little, it may be
As with jokes about his family
The rough hands tease him merrily.

But lightly, gayly as he replies,
A braver, prouder light in his eyes,
Shows that he loves and can guard his prize.

And the voice o'er the roar of the mill-wheel heard,
In the house is as soft in every word,
As if the wife were some timid bird ;

And he strokes her hair as we handle such
Dear things, that we love to pet, so much
And yet are half afraid to touch.

And Bethy, pretty, young, and gay,
Trying the strange new matron way,
Seems to " make believe," like a child at play.

ın and out the whole day long
At work in the house, or her flowers among,
You scarce can hear the bırds for her song.

Though many times does she steal, I ween,
A glance at the mill, the blinds between,
Blushing, and careful not to be seen,

But busy with sewing, broom, or meal,
Swiftly away the moments steal,
And she hears the last slow turn of the wheel.

And the miller glad, but tired and slow,
Comes, looking white as the man of snow
They made in the winter, long ago.

Oft the cottage door is opened wide,
Before his hand the latch has tried,
By the eager wife who waits inside.

Though sometimes out from a hiding-place,
She slyly peeps, when he comes, to trace
The puzzled wonder of his face.

And she loves to see the glad surprise,
That, when from her secret nook she flies,
Shines in his happy, laughing eyes.

And he, before from his hand she slips,
Leaves the mark on her waist of finger tips,
And powders her pretty face and lips.

THE BABY.

O'er the miller's cottage the seasons glide,
And at the next year's Christmas-tide
We see her a mother, we saw a bride.

All in the Spring was the brown flax spun,
All in the Summer it bleached in the sun ;
In the autumn days was the sewing done.

And just when the Babe was born of old,
Close wrapped in many a dainty fold,
She gave the mother her babe to hold.

Ah, sweetly the maiden's ditties rung,
And sweet was the song the young wife sung
But never trembled yet on her tongue,

Such tender notes as the lullabies,
That now beside the cradle rise
Where softly sleeping the baby lies.

And the child has made the father grow
Prouder, as all who see may know,
Than he was of his bride, a year ago.

He kinder too has grown to all,
And oft as the gloomy shadows fall,
He speaks of the Squire in his lonely hall.

And Bethy, even more tender grown,
Says, almost with tears in her tone,
How he's growing old in his home alone.

For now, that her life is so bright and fair,
She thinks of all men with griefs to bear ;
And of sorrowful women everywhere,

Who sit with empty hands to hold,
And weep for babies dead and cold, —
And of such as never had babes to hold.

So the miller and wife live on in their cot
Untroubled, content with what they have got ; —
Hath the whole wide world a happier lot?

And the neighbors all about declare,
That never a better, handsomer pair,
Are seen at market, church, or fair.

So free from envy, pride, or guile,
They keep their rustic simple style,
And bask in fortune's kindliest smile,

Though time and tide must go as they will,
And change must even cross the sill
Of the happy Miller of Dovecote Mill.

13

THE FATHER.

Hushed is the even-song of the bird,
Naught but the katydid is heard,
And the sound of leaves by the night wind stirred

Swarms of fireflies rise and shine
Out of the green grass, short and fine,
Where, dotting the meadows, sleep the kine.

And the bees, done flying to and fro,
In the fields of buckwheat, white as snow,
Cling to the hive, in a long black row.

Closed are the pink and the poppy red,
And the lily near them hangs her head,
And the camomile sleeps on the garden bed.

The wheel is still that has turned all day,
And the mill stream runs unvexed away,
Under the thin mist, cool and gray,

And the little vine-clad home in the dell
With this quiet beauty suiteth well,
For it seems a place where peace should dwell

And sitting to-night on the cottage sill
Is the wife of the Miller of Dovecote Mill, —
Quiet Bethy, thoughtful and still.

As she hears the cricket chirping low,
And the pendulum swinging to and fro,
And the child in the cradle, breathing slow ;

Are her thoughts with her baby, fast asleep,
Or do they wander away, and keep
With him she waits for as night grows deep ? .

Or are they back to the days gone by,
When free as the birds that swing and fly,
She lived with never a care or tie?

Ah ! who of us all has ever known
The hidden thought and the undertone
Of the bosom nearest to our own !

For the one we deemed devoid of art
May have lain and dreamed on our trusting heart
The dreams in which we had no part !

And Bethy, the honest miller's wife,
Whom he loves as he loves his very life,
May be with him and herself at strife.

For she was only a child that day,
When she gave her hand in the church away,
And the friends who loved her used to say, —

(For you know she was the country's pride,)
If she ever had had a suitor beside
She might not be such a willing bride !

Though never one would hint but he
Was as true and good and fair as she,
They wondered still that the match should be,

And said, were she like a lady drest,
There was not a fairer, east nor west; —
And yet it might be all for the best! ·

So who can guess her thoughts as her sight
Rests on the road-track, dusty and white,
The way the miller must come to-night!

———

Up in his gloomy house on the hill,
He lies in his chamber, white and still, —
The Squire, who owns the Dovecote Mill.

What hath the rich man been in his day?
" Hard and cruel and stern, alway ; " —
This is the thing his neighbors say,

" Silent and grim as a man could be; " —
But the miller's wife, says, tenderly,
" He has always a smile for the babe and me."

But whatever he was, in days gone by,
Let us stand in his presence reverently,
For to him the great change draweth nigh.

There the light is dim, and the June winds blow
The heavy curtains, to and fro,
And the watchers, near him, whisper low.

Something the sick man asks from his bed;
Is it the leach or the priest? they said.
" Nay, bring me Bethy, here," he said.

" Have you not heard me; will you not heed;
Go to the miller's wife with speed,
And tell her the dying of her hath need."

Slowly the watchers shook the head,
They knew that his poor wits wanderèd;
" Yet, now let him have his way," they said.

So when the turn of the night has come,
She stands at his bedside, frightened, dumb,
Holding his fingers, cold and numb.

He has sent the watchers and nurse away,
And now he is keeping death at bay,
Till he rids his soul of what he would say.

" Now, hear me, Bethy, I am not wild,
As I hope to God to be reconciled,
I am thy father — thou my child!

" I loved a maiden, the noblest one
That ever the good sun shone upon:
I had wealth and honors, she had none.

" And when I wooed her, she answered me, —
' Nay, I am too humble to wed with thee,
Let me rather thine handmaid be!'

" From home with me, for love, she fled
The night that in secret we were wed;
And she kept the secret, living and dead.

" Serving for wages duly paid,
In my home she lived, as an humble maid,
Till under the grass of the churchyard laid.

" Twenty years has remorse been fed,
Twenty years has she lain there dead,
With her sweet name, Mercy, at her head.

" How you came to the world was known
But to the gardener's wife alone,
Who took, and reared you up as her own.

" Though conscience whispered, early and late,
Your child is worthy a higher fate,
Still shame and pride said, always, wait.

" But alas! a debt unpaid grows vast.
And whether it come, or slow or fast,
The day of reckoning comes at last.

" So, all there was left to do, I have done,
And the gold and the acres I have won
Shall come to you with the morning's sun.

" And may this atone; oh would that it might,
And lessen the guilt of my soul to-night,
For the one great wrong that I cannot right."

Scarcely the daughter breathed or stirred,
As she listened close for another word;
But "Mercy!" was all that she ever heard

She clung to his breast, she bade him stay,
But ere the words to her lips found way,
She knew the thing that she held was clay.

All that she had was a father's gold,
Never his kind warm hand to hold,
Never a kiss till his lips were cold!

THE WIFE.

Brightly the morning sunshine glowed,
As slowly, thoughtfully, Bethy trode,
Towards the mill by the winter road.

Now she sees the mansion proud and gray,
And its goodly acres stretching away,
And she knows that these are hers to-day.

Glad visions surely before her rise,
For bright in her cheek the color lies,
And a strange new light in her tender eyes.

Now she is rich, and a lady born,
Does she think of her last year's wedding morn,
And the house where she came a bride, with scorn?

And to him, unfit for a lady, grand,
To whom she gave her willing hand,
Though he brought her neither house nor land?

How will she meet him? what is his fate,
Who eager leans o'er the rustic gate
To watch her coming?   Hush and wait!

No word she says as over the sill,
And into the cottage low and still,
She walks by the Miller of Dovecote Mill.

Why does she tremble, the goodman's dame,
And turn away as she speaks his name?
Is it for love, or alas! for shame?

" Last night," she says, "as I watched for thee,
Came those from the great house hurriedly,
Who said that the master sent for me:

" That his life was burned to a feeble flame,
But sleeping or waking all the same,
And day and night he called my name.

" So I followed wondering, where they led,
And half bewildered, half in dread,
I stood at midnight by his bed.

" What matter, to tell what he said again;
The dreams perchance of a wandering brain!
Only one thing is sure and plain.

"Of his gold and land and houses fine,
  All that he had, to-day is thine,
  Since in dying he made them mine.

"I would that the gift were in thy name,
  Yet mine or thine it is all the same;
  And we must not speak of the dead with blame.

"And who but thee should be his heir?
  Thou hast served him ever with faithful care,
  And he had no son his name to bear!"

Slowly, as one who marveled still,
  Answered the Miller of Dovecote Mill,
"'Tis a puzzle, tell it how you will,

"Why his child could never better fare
  Than thou, with wealth enough and to spare.
  For it is not I but thou who art heir.

"'Tis not so strange it should come to thee,
  Thou wert fit for a lady, as all could see,
  And rich or poor, too good for me."

Meek before him she bowed her head;
"I want nor honor nor gold," she said,
"I take my lot as it is instead.

"Keep gold and lands and houses fine,
  But give me thy love, as I give thee mine,
  And my wealth shall still be more than thine!

" And if I had been in a mansion bred,
  And not in a humble cot," she said,
" I think we two should still have wed.

" For if I had owned the acres grand,
  Instead of the gardener's scanty land,
  I had given them all for thy heart and hand.

" So, heiress or lady, what you will,
  This only title I covet still,
  Wife of the Miller of Dovecote Mill!"

A BALLAD OF LAUDERDALE.

A SHEPHERD's child young Barbara grew,
  A wild flower of the vale;
While gallant Duncan was the heir
  Of the Laird of Lauderdale.

He sat at ease in bower and hall
  With ladies gay and fine;
She led her father's sheep at morn,
  At eve she milked the kine.

O'er field and fell his steed he rode,
  The foremost in the race;
She bounded graceful as the deer
  He followed in the chase.

Yet oft he left his pleasant friends,
 And, musing, walked apart;
For vague unrest and soft desire
 Were stirring in his heart.

One morn, when others merrily
 Wound horn within the wood,
He on the hillside strayed alone,
 In tender, thoughtful mood.

And there, with yellow snooded hair,
 And plaid about her flung,
Tending her pretty flock of sheep,
 Fair Barbara sat and sung.

The very heath-flower bent to hear,
 The echoes seemed to pause,
As sweet and clear the maiden sang
 The song of " Leader Haughs."

And, while young Duncan, gazing, stood
 Enchanted by the sound,
He from the arrows of her eyes
 Received a mortal wound !

" Sweet maid," he cried, " the first whose power
 Hath ever held me fast;
Now take my love, or scorn my love,
 You still shall be the last ! "

She felt her heart with pity move,
 Yet hope within her died ;
She knew her friendless poverty,
 She knew his wealth and pride.

"Alas! your father's scorn," she said.
 "Alas! my humble state."
"'Twere pity," Duncan gayly cried,
 But love were strong as hate!"

He took her little trembling hand,
 He kissed her fears away;
"Whate'er the morrow brings," he said,
 "We'll live and love to-day!"

So all the Summer through they met,
 Nor thought what might betide,
Till the purple heather all about
 The hills grew brown and died.

One eve they, parting, lingered long
 Together in the dell,
When suddenly a shadow black
 As fate between them fell.

The hot blood rushed to Duncan's brow,
 The maiden's cheek grew pale,
For right across their pathway frowned
 The Laird of Lauderdale.

Ah! cruel was the word he spake,
 And cruel was his deed;
He would not see the maiden's face,
 Nor hear the lover plead.

He called his followers, in wrath,
 They came in haste and fright;
They tore the youth from out her arms,
 . They bore him from her sight.

And he at eve may come no more;
  Her song no more she trills;
Her cheek is whiter than the lambs
  She leads along the hills.

For Barbara now is left alone
  Through all the weary hours,
While Duncan pines a prisoner, fast
  Within his father's towers.

And Autumn goes, and Spring-time comes,
  And Duncan, true and bold,
Has scorned alike his father's threats'
  And bribes of land and gold.

And Autumn goes, and Spring-time comes,
  And Barbara sings and smiles:
" 'Tis fair for love," she softly says,
  " To use love's arts and wiles."

No other counselor hath she
  But her own sweet constancy;
Yet hath her wit devised a way
  To set her true love free.

One night, when slumber brooded deep
  O'er all the peaceful glen,
She baked a cake, the like of which
  Was never baked till then.

For first she took a slender cord,
  And wound it close and small;
Then in the barley bannock safe
  She hid the mystic ball.

Next morn her father missed his child,
  He searched the valley round ;
But not a maid like her within
  Twice twenty miles was found.

For she hath ta'en the maiden snood
  And the bright curls from her head,
And now she wears the bonnet blue
  Of a shepherd lad instead.

And she hath crossed the silent hills,
  And crossed the lonely vale ;
And safe at morn she stands before
  The towers of Lauderdale.

And not a hand is raised to harm
  The pretty youth and tall,
With just a bannock in his scrip,
  Who stands without the wall.

Careless awhile *he* wanders round,
  But when the daylight dies
He comes and stands beneath the tower
  Where faithful Duncan lies.

Fond man ! nor sunset dyes he sees,
  Nor stars come out above ;
His thoughts are all upon the hills,
  ·Where first he learned to love ;

When suddenly he hears a voice,
  That makes his pulses start —
A sweet voice singing " Leader Haughs,"
  The song that won his heart.

He leans across the casement high ;
    A minstrel boy he spies ;
He knows the maiden of his love
    Through all her strange disguise !.

She made a sign, she spake no word,
    And never a word spake he ;
She took the bannock from her scrip
    And brake it on her knee ;

She threw the slender cord aloft,
    He caught and made it fast ;
One moment more and he is safe,
    Free as the winds at last !

No time is this for speech or kiss,
    No time for aught but flight ;
His good steed standing in the stall
    Must bear them far to-night.

So swiftly Duncan brought him forth,
    He mounted hastily ;
" Now, set your foot on mine," he said,
    " And give your hand to me ! "

He lifts her up ; they sweep the hills,
    They ford the foaming beck ;
He kisses soft the loving hands
    That cling about his neck.

In vain at morn the Laird, in wrath,
    Would follow where they fled ;
They're o'er the Border, far away,
    Before the east is red.

And when the third day's sun at eve
  Puts on his purple state
Brave Duncan checks his foaming steed
  Before his father's gate.

Out came the Laird, with cruel look,
  With quick and angry stride;
When at his feet down knelt his son,
  With Barbara at his side.

" Forgive me, father," low he said,
  No single word she spake;
But the tender face she lifted up
  Plead for her lover's sake.

She raised to him her trembling hands,
  In her eyes the tears were bright,
And any but a heart of stone
  Had melted at the sight.

" Let love," cried Duncan, " bear the blame,
  Love would not be denied;
Fast were we wedded yestermorn,
  I bring you here my bride ! "

Then the Laird looked down into her eyes,
  And his tears were near to fall;
He raised them both from off the ground,
  He led them toward the Hall.

Wondering the mute retainers stood,
  " Why give you not," he said,
" The homage due unto my son,
  And to her whom he hath wed ? "

Then every knee was lowly bent,
  And every head was bare ;
" Long live," they cried, " his fair young bride,
  And our master's honored heir ! "

Years come and go, and in his stall
  The good steed idly stånds ;
The Laird is laid with his line to rest,
  By his children's loving hands.

And now within the castle proud
  They lead a happy life ;
For he is Laird of Lauderdale,
  And she his Lady wife.

And oft, when hand in hand they sit,
  And watch the day depart,
She sings the song of " Leader Haughs,"
  The song that won his heart !

THE THREE WRENS.

Mr. Wren and his dear began early one year —
  They were married, of course, on St. Valentine's
    day, —
To build such a nest as was safest and best,
  And to get it all finished and ready by May.

Their house, snug and fine, they set up in a vine,
  That sheltered a cottage from sunshine and heat :
14

Mrs. Wren said : " I am sure, this is nice and secure;
   And besides, I can see in the house, or the street."

Mr. Wren, who began, like a wise married man,
   To check his mate's weak inclination to roam,
Shook his little brown head, and reprovingly said :
   " My dear, you had better be looking at home.

" You'll be trying the street pretty soon with your feet,
   And neglecting your house and my comfort, no
      doubt,
And you'll find a pretext for a call on them next,
   If you watch to see what other folks are about.

" There's your own home to see, and besides there is
   me,
   And this visiting neighbors is nonsense and stuff!
You would like to know why ? well, you'd better not
      try ; —
   I don't choose to have you, and that is enough ! "

Mrs. Wren did not say she would have her own
   way, —
   In fact, she seemed wonderfully meek and serene;
But she thought, I am sure, though she looked so
   demure,
   " Well I don't care; I think you're most awfully
   mean ! "

Mr. Wren soon flew off, thinking, likely enough,
   I could manage a dozen such creatures with ease ;
She began to reflect, I see what you expect,
   But if I know myself, I shall look where I please !

However, at night, when he came from his flight,
    Both acted as if there was nothing amiss:
Put a wing o'er their head, and went chirping to bed,
    To dream of a summer of sunshine and bliss.

I need scarcely remark, they were up with the lark,
    And by noon they were tired of work without play ;
And thought it was best for the present to rest,
    And then finish their task in the cool of the day.

So, concealed by the leaves that grew thick to the
    eaves,
    He shut himself in, and he shut the world out ; —
" Now," said she, " he's asleep, I will just take a peep
    In the cottage, and see what the folks are about."

Then she looked very sly, from her perch safe and
    high,
    Through the great open window, left wide for the
    sun ;
And she said : " I can't see what the danger can be,
    I am sure here is nothing to fear or to shun !

" There's an old stupid cat, half asleep on the mat,
    But I think she's too lazy to stir or to walk ; —
Oh, you just want to show your importance, I know.
    But you can't frighten me, Mr. Wren, with your
    talk !

" Now to have my own will, I'll step down on that
    sill ;
    I'm not an inquisitive person — oh, no ;
I don't want to see what's improper for me,
    But I like to find out for myself that it's so."

Then this rash little wren hopped on further again,
  And grown bolder, flew in, and sat perched on a
    chair ;
Saying, " What there is here that is dreadful or
    queer,
  I haven't been able to find, I declare.

" Well, I wish for your sake, Mr. Wren, you would
    wake,
  And see what effect all your warning has had ;
Ah! I'll call up that cat, and we'll have a nice chat,
  And rouse him with talking — oh, won't he be
    mad ! "

So she cried, loud and clear, " Good-day, Tabby, my
    dear !
  I think neighbors a neighborly feeling should
    show."
" How your friendliness charms," said Puss ; " come to
    my arms,
  I have had my eye on you some time, do you
    know ! "

Something like a sharp snap broke that moment his
    nap,
  And Mr. Wren said, with a stretch and a wink :
" I suppose, dear, your sleep has been tranquil and deep ;
  I just lost myself for a moment, I think.

" Why! she's gone, I declare ! well, I'd like to know
    where ? "
  And his head up and down peering round him he
    dips ;

All he saw in the gloom of the shadowy room,
  Was an innocent cat meekly licking her lips !

" 'Tis too bad she's away ; for, of course, I can't stay,"
  Said the great Mr. Wren, " shut in this little space :
We must come and must go, but these females, you
    know,
  Never need any changes of work or of place."

And then he began, like a badly-used man,
  To twitter and chirp with an impatient cry ;
But soon pausing, sang out, " She's gone off in a pout,
  But if she prefers being alone, so do I !

" Yet the place is quite still, so I'll whistle until
  She returns to her home full of shame and remorse ;
I'm not lonesome at all, but it's no harm to call ;
  She'll come back fast enough when she hears me, of
    course ! "

So he started his tune, but broke off very soon,
  As if he'd been wasting his time, like a dunce ;
For he suddenly caught at a very wise thought,
  And he altered his whole plan of action at once.

" Now, that cat," he exclaimed, " may be wrongfully
    blamed ;
  And since it's a delicate matter to broach,
I don't say of her, that she is not *sans peur*,
  But I'm sure in this matter she's not *sans reproche !*

" Ah ! I can't love a wren, as I loved her, again,
  But I'll try to be manly and act as I ought ;

And the birds in the trees, like the fish in the seas,
    May be just as good ones as ever were caught.

" And if one in the hand, as all men understand,
    Is worth two in the bush," Mr. Wren gravely said,
" Then it seems to me plain, by that same rule again,
    That a bird in the bush is worth two that are dead."

So he dropped his sad note, and he smoothed down his
        coat,
    Till his late-ruffled plumage shone glossy and bright;
And light as a breeze, through the fields and the trees,
    He floated and carolled till lost to the sight.

And in no longer time than it takes for my rhyme, —
    Now, would you believe it ? and isn't it strange ! —
He returned all elate, bringing home a new mate :
    But birds are but birds, and are given to change.

Of course, larger folks are quite crushed by such
        strokes,
    And never are guilty of like fickle freaks ; —
Ah ! a bird's woe is brief, but our great human grief
    Will sometimes affect us for days and for weeks !

But this does not belong of good right to my song,
    For I started to tell about birds and their kind ;
So I'll say Mr. Wren, when he married again,
    Took a wife who had not an inquiring mind.

For he said what was true : " Mrs. Wren, number
        two,
    You would not have had such good fortune, my
        dear,

If the first, who is dead, had believed what I said,
    And contented herself in her own proper sphere.'

Now, to some it might seem like the very extreme
    Of folly to ask what you know very well ;
But this Mrs. Wren did, and behaved as he bid,
    Never asking the wherefore, and he didn't tell.

Yes, this meek little bird never thought, never stirred,
    Without craving leave in the properest way :
She said, with the rest, " Shall I sit on my nest
    For three weeks or thirteen ? I'll do just as you
      say ! "

Now I think, in the main, it is best to explain
    The right and the reason of what we command ;
But he wouldn't, not he ; a poor female was she,
    And he was a male bird as large as your hand !

And one more thing, I find, is borne in on my mind :
    Mr. Wren may be right, but it seems to me strange,
That while both his grief and his love were so brief,
    He should claim such devotion and trust in ex-
      change !

And yet I've been told, that with birds young and old,
    All the males should direct, all the females obey ;
Though, to speak for a bird, so at least I have heard,
    You must *be* one :—as I never was, I can't say !

DOROTHY'S DOWER.

IN THREE PARTS.

PART I.

"My sweetest Dorothy," said John,
  Of course before the wedding,
As metaphorically he stood,
  His gold upon her shedding,
"Whatever thing you wish or want
  Shall be hereafter granted,
For all my worldly goods are yours."
  The fellow was enchanted!

"About that little dower you have,
  You thought might yet come handy,
Throw it away, do what you please,
  Spend it on sugar-candy!
I like your sweet, dependent ways,
  I love you when you tease me;
The more you ask, the more you spend,
  The better you will please me."

PART II.

"Confound it, Dorothy!" said John,
  "I haven't got it by me.
You haven't, have you, spent that sum,
  The dower from Aunt Jemima?
No; well that's sensible for you;
  This fix is most unpleasant;
But money's tight, so just take yours
  And use it for the present.

Now I must go — to — meet a man !
By George ! I'll have to borrow !
Lend me a twenty — that's all right !
I'll pay you back to-morrow."

PART III.

" Madame," says John to Dorothy,
And past her rudely pushes,
" You think a man is made of gold,
And money grows on bushes !
Tom's shoes ! your doctor !   Can't you now
Get up some new disaster ?
You and your children are enough
To break John Jacob Astor.
Where's what you had yourself when I
Was fool enough to court you ?
That little sum, till you got me,
'Twas what had to support you ! "
" It's lent and gone, not very far ;
Pray don't be apprehensive."
" *Lent !*   I've had use enough for it :
My family is expensive.
I didn't, as a woman would,
Spend it on sugar-candy ! "
" No, John, I think the most of it
Went for cigars and brandy ! "

BLACK RANALD.

In the time when the little flowers are born,
   The joyfulest time of the year,
Fair Marion from the Hall rode forth
   To chase the fleet red deer.

She moved among her comely maids
   With such a stately mein
That they seemed like humble violets
   By the side of a lily queen.

For she, of beauties fair, was named
   The fairest in the land ;
And lovelorn youths had pined and died
   For the clasp of her lady hand.

But never suitor yet had pressed
   Her dainty finger-tips ;
And never cheek that wore a beard
   Had touched her maiden lips.

She laughed and danced, she laughed and sang ;
   She bade her lovers wait ;
Till the gallant Stuart Græme, one morn,
   Checked rein at her father's gate.

She blushed and sighed ; she laughed no more ;
   She sang a low refrain ;
And, when the bold young Stuart wooed,
   He did not woo in vain.

And now, as to the chase she rides,
　　Across her father's land,
She wears a bright betrothal ring
　　Upon her snowy hand.

She loosed the rein, she touched the flank
　　Of her royal, red-roan steed.
" Now, who among my friends," she said,
　　" Will vie with me in speed ? "

She looked at Græme before them all,
　　Though her face was rosy red.
" He who can catch me as I ride
　　Shall be my squire," she said.

Away ! they scarce can follow her,
　　Even with their eager eyes ;
She clears the stream, she skims the plain
　　Swift as the swallow flies.

Alack ! no charger in the train
　　Can match with hers to-day ;
The very deer-hounds, left behind,
　　Are yelling in dismay.

Far out upon the lonely moor
　　Her speed she checks at last ;
One single horseman follows her,
　　With hoof-strokes gaining fast.

She's smiling softly to herself,
　　She's speaking soft and low :
" None but the gallant Stuart Græme
　　Could follow where I go ! "

She wheels her horse; she sees a sight
   That makes her pulses stand;
Her very cheek, but now so red,
   Grows whiter than her hand.

For, while no friend she sees the way
   Her frightened eyes look back,
Black Ranald, of the Haunted Tower,
   Is close upon her track!

He's gained her side; he's seized her rein —
   The cruelest man in the land;
And he has clasped her virgin waist
   With his wicked, wicked hand.

She feels his breath upon her face,
   She hears his mocking tone,
As he lifts her from her red-roan steed
   And sets her on his own.

" Proud Mistress Marion," he cries,
   " In spite of all your scorn,
Black Ranald is your squire to-day,
   He'll be your lord at morn!"

She hears no more, she sees no more,
   For many a weary hour,
Till from her deadly swoon she wakes
   In Ranald's Haunted Tower.

For, in the highest turret there,
   With never a friend in call,
He has tied her hands with a silver chain
   And bound them to the wall.

She fears no ghosts that haunt the dark,
  But she fears the coming dawn ;
And her heart grows sick when at day she hears
  The prison-bolts withdrawn.

She summons all her strength, as they
  Who for the headsman wait ;
And she prays to every virgin saint
  To help her in her strait ;

For she sees her jailer cross the sill.
  " Now, if you will wed with me,"
He said, " henceforth of my house and land
  You shall queen and ruler be."

" Bold Ranald of the Tower," she said,
  "With heart as black as your name,
I will only be the bride of Death
  Or the bride of Stuart Græme.

" I will make the coldest, darkest bed
  In the dismal churchyard mine,
And lay me down to sleep in it,
  Or ever I sleep in thine ! "

" I shall tame you yet, proud girl," he cried,
  " For you shall not be free,
Nor bread nor wine shall pass your lips
  Till you vow to wed with me ! "

She turned ; she laughed in his very face :
  " Sir Knave, your threats are vain ;
Nor bread nor wine shall pass my lips
  Till I am free again ! "

He echoed back her mocking laugh,
 He turned him on his heel ;
When something smote upon his ear
 Like the ringing clang of steel.

The bolts are snapped ; the strong door falls ;
 The Græme is standing there ;
And a hundred armèd men at his back
 Are swarming up the stair !

Black Ranald put his horn to his lips
 And blew a warning note.
" Your followers lie," brave Stuart said,
 " Six deep within the moat !

" Alone, a prisoner in your tower,
 Now yield, or you are dead ! "
Black Ranald gnashed his teeth in rage.
 " I yield to none," he said.

They drew their swords. " Now die the death,"
 Said Græme, " you merit well."
And as he spake at Marion's feet
 The lifeless Ranald fell.

The Stuart raised the death-pale maid ;
 He broke her silver chain ;
He bore her down, and set her safe
 On her good red-roan again.

Now closely at his side she rides,
 Nor heeds them one and all ;
And his hand ne'er quits her bridle-rein
 Till they reach her father's Hall.

Then the glad sire clasps that hand in his own,
  While the tears to his beard drop slow :
" You have saved my child and rid the land,"
  He cries, " of a cruel foe ;

" And if this maiden say not nay," —
  Her cheeks burned like a flame, —
" Then you shall be my son to-night,
  And she shall bear your name."

They have set the lights in every room ;
  They have spread the wedding-feast ;
And from the neighboring cloister's cell
  They have brought the holy priest.

And she is a captive once again —
  The timid, tender dove !
For she slipped the silver chain to wear
  The golden chain of love !

Sweet Marion, under her snow-white veil,
  Stands fast by her captor's side,
As he binds her hands with the marriage-ring
  And kisses her first, a bride !

THE LEAK IN THE DIKE.

A STORY OF HOLLAND.

THE good dame looked from her cottage
  At the close of the pleasant day,
And cheerily called to her little son
  Outside the door at play:

" Come, Peter, come ! I want you to go,
  While there is light to see,
To the hut of the blind old man who lives
  Across the dike, for me ;
And take these cakes I made for him —
  They are hot and smoking yet ;
You have time enough to go and come
  Before the sun is set."

Then the good-wife turned to her labor,
  Humming a simple song,
And thought of her husband, working hard
  At the sluices all day long ;
And set the turf a-blazing,
  And brought the coarse black bread ;
That he might find a fire at night,
  And find the table spread.

And Peter left the brother,
  With whom all day he had played,
And the sister who had watched their sports
  In the willow's tender shade ;
And told them they'd see him back before
  They saw a star in sight,
Though he wouldn't be afraid to go
  In the very darkest night !
For he was a brave, bright fellow,
  With eye and conscience clear ;
He could do whatever a boy might do,
  And he had not learned to fear.
Why, he wouldn't have robbed a bird's nest,
  Nor brought a stork to harm,
Though never a law in Holland
  Had stood to stay his arm !

And now, with his face all glowing,
   And eyes as bright as the day
With the thoughts of his pleasant errand,
   He trudged along the way ;
And soon his joyous prattle
   Made glad a lonesome place —
Alas ! if only the blind old man
   Could have seen that happy face !
Yet he somehow caught the brightness
   Which his voice and presence lent ;
And he felt the sunshine come and go
   As Peter came and went.

And now, as the day was sinking,
   And the winds began to rise,
The mother looked from her door again,
   Shading her anxious eyes ;
And saw the shadows deepen,
   And birds to their homes come back,
But never a sign of Peter
   Along the level track.
But she said : " He will come at morning,
   So I need not fret or grieve —
Though it isn't like my boy at all
   To stay without my leave."

But where was the child delaying ?
   On the homeward way was he,
And across the dike while the sun was up
   An hour above the sea.
He was stopping now to gather flowers,
   Now listening to the sound,

15

As the angry waters dashed themselves
  Against their narrow bound.
" Ah ! well for us," said Peter,
  " That the gates are good and strong,
And my father tends them carefully,
  Or they would not hold you long !
" You're a wicked sea," said Peter ;
  " I know why you fret and chafe ;
You would like to spoil our lands and homes ;
  But our sluices keep you safe ! "

But hark ! Through the noise of waters
  Comes a low, clear, trickling sound ;
And the child's face pales with terror,
  And his blossoms drop to the ground.
He is up the bank in a moment,
  And, stealing through the sand,
He sees a stream not yet so large
  As his slender, childish hand.
'Tis a leak in the dike ! He is but a boy,
  Unused to fearful scenes ;
But, young as he is, he has learned to know
  The dreadful thing that means.
A leak in the dike ! The stoutest heart
  Grows faint that cry to hear,
And the bravest man in all the land
  Turns white with mortal fear.
For he knows the smallest leak may grow
  To a flood in a single night ;
And he knows the strength of the cruel sea
  When loosed in its angry might.

And the boy ! He has seen the danger,
  And, shouting a wild alarm,

He forces back the weight of the sea
  With the strength of his single arm !
He listens for the joyful sound
  Of a footstep passing nigh ;
And lays his ear to the ground, to catch
  The answer to his cry.
And he hears the rough winds blowing,
  And the waters rise and fall,
But never an answer comes to him,
  Save the echo of his call.
He sees no hope, no succor,
  His feeble voice is lost ;
Yet what shall he do but watch and wait,
  Though he perish at his post !

So, faintly calling and crying
  Till the sun is under the sea ;
Crying and moaning till the stars
  Come out for company ;
He thinks of his brother and sister,
  Asleep in their safe warm bed ;
He thinks of his father and mother,
  Of himself as dying — and dead ;
And of how, when the night is over,
  They must come and find him at last :
But he never thinks he can leave the place
  Where duty holds him fast.

The good dame in the cottage
  Is up and astir with the light,
For the thought of her little Peter
  Has been with her all night.
And now she watches the pathway,
  As yestereve she had done ;

But what does she see so strange and black
  Against the rising sun ?
Her neighbors are bearing between them
  Something straight to her door ;
Her child is coming home, but not
  As he ever came before !

"He is dead ! " she cries ; " my darling ! "
  And the startled father hears,
And comes and looks the way she looks,
  And fears the thing she fears :
Till a glad shout from the bearers
  Thrills the stricken man and wife —
" Give thanks, for your son has saved our land,
  And God has saved his life ! "
So, there in the morning sunshine
  They knelt about the boy ;
And every head was bared and bent
  In tearful, reverent joy.

'Tis many a year since then ; but still,
  When the sea roars like a flood,
Their boys are taught what a boy can do
  Who is brave and true and good.
For every man in that country
  Takes his son by the hand,
And tells him of little Peter,
  Whose courage saved the land.

They have many a valiant hero,
  Remembered through the years ;
But never one whose name so oft
  Is named with loving tears.

And his deed shall be sung by the cradle,
And told to the child on the knee,
So long as the dikes of Holland
Divide the land from the sea !

THE LANDLORD OF THE BLUE HEN.

ONCE, a long time ago, so good stories begin,
There stood by the roadside an old-fashioned inn ;
An inn, which the landlord had named " The Blue
Hen,"
While he, by his neighbors, was called " Uncle Ben ;

At least, they quite often addressed him that way
When ready to drink but not ready to pay ;
Though when he insisted on having the cash,
They went off, muttering " Rummy," and " Old Brandy
Smash."

He sold barrels of liquor, but still the old " Hen "
Seemed never to flourish, and neither did " Ben ; "
For he drank up his profits, as every one knew,
Ever those who were drinking their profits up, too.

So, with all they could drink, and with all they could
pay,
The landlord grew poorer and poorer each day ;
Men said, as he took down the gin from the shelf,
" The steadiest customer there was himself."

There was hardly a man living in the same street
But had too much to drink and too little to eat ;

The women about the old " Hen " got the *blues ;*
The girls had no bonnets, the boys had no shoes.

When a poor fellow died, he was borne on his bier
By his comrades, whose hands shook with brandy and
    fear ;
For of course, they were terribly frightened, and yet,
They went back to " The Blue Hen " to drink and
    forget !

There was one jovial farmer who couldn't get by
The door of " The Blue Hen " without feeling dry ;
One day he discovered his purse growing light,
" There must be a leak somewhere," he said.   He was
    right !

Then there was the blacksmith (the best ever known
Folks said, if he'd only let liquor alone)
Let his forge cool so often, at last he forgot
To heat up his iron and strike when 'twas hot.

Once a miller, going home from " The Blue Hen,"
    'twas said,
While his wife sat and wept by his sick baby's bed,
Had made a false step, and slept all night alone
In the bed of the river, instead of his own.

Even poor " Ben " himself could not drink of the cup
Of fire forever without burning up ;
He grew sick, fell to raving, declared that he knew
No doctors could help him ; and they said so, too.

He told those about him, the ghosts of the men
Who used in their life-times to haunt " The Blue Hen,

Had come back each one bringing his children and
    wife,
And trying to frighten him out of his life.

Now he thought he was burning; the very next breath
He shivered and cried, he was freezing to death;
That the peddler lay by him, who, long years ago,
Was put out of " The Blue Hen," and died in the
    snow.

He said that the blacksmith who turned to a sot,
Laid him out on an anvil and beat him, red-hot;
That the builder, who swallowed his brandy fourth
    proof,
Was pitching him downward, head first, from the roof.

At last he grew frantic; he clutched at the sheet,
And cried that the miller had hold of his feet;
Then leaped from his bed with a terrible scream,
That the dead man was dragging him under the stream.

Then he ran, and so swift that no mortal could save;
He went over the bank and went under the wave;
And his poor lifeless body next morning was found
In the very same spot where the miller was drowned.

" 'Twasn't liquor that killed him," some said, " that was
    plain;
He was crazy, and sober folks might be insane!"
" 'Twas *delirium tremens*," the coroner said,
But whatever it was, he was certainly dead!

THE KING'S JEWEL.

'Twas a night to make the bravest
　. Shrink from the tempest's breath,
For the winter snows were bitter,
　And the winds were cruel as death

All day on the roofs of Warsaw
　Had the white storm sifted down
Till it almost hid the humble huts
　Of the poor, outside the town.

And it beat upon one low cottage
　With a sort of reckless spite
As if to add to their wretchedness
　Who sat by its hearth that night;

Where Dorby, the Polish peasant,
　Took his pale wife by the hand,
And told her that when the morrow came
　They would have no home in the land.

No human hand would aid him
　With the rent that was due at morn;
And his cold, hard-hearted landlord
　Had spurned his prayers with scorn.

Then the poor man took his Bible,
　And read, while his eyes grew dim,
To see if any comfort
　Were written there for him;

When he suddenly heard a knocking
   On the casement, soft and light;
It wasn't the storm; but what else could be
   Abroad in such a night?

Then he went and opened the window,
   But for wonder scarce could speak,
As a bird flew in with a jeweled ring
   Held flashing in his beak.

'Tis the bird I trained, said Dorby,
   And that is the precious ring,
That once I saw on the royal hand
   Of our good and gracious King.

And if birds, as our lesson tells us,
   Once came with food to men,
Who knows, said the foolish peasant,
   But they might be sent again!

So he hopefully went with the morning,
   And knocked at the palace gate,
And gave to the King the jewel
   They had searched for long and late.

And when he had heard the story,
   Which the peasant had to tell;
He gave him a fruitful garden,
   And a home wherein to dwell.

And Dorby wrote o'er the doorway
   These words that all might see:
" Thou hast called on the Lord in trouble,
   And He hath delivered thee!"

EDGAR'S WIFE.

I KNOW that Edgar's kind and good,
  And I know my home is fine,
If I only could live in it, mother,
  And only could make it mine.

You need not look at me and smile,
  In such a strange, sad way;
I am not out of my head at all,
  And I know just what I say.

I know that Edgar freely gives
  Whate'er he thinks will please;
But it's what we love that brings us good,
  And my heart is not in these.

Oh, I wish I could stand where the maples
  Drop their shadows, cool and dim;
Or lie in the sweet red clover,
  Where I walked, but not with him!

Nay, you need not mind me, mother,
  I love him — or at the worst,
I try to shut the past from my heart;
  But you know he was not the first!

And I strive to make him feel my life
  Is his, and here, as I ought;
But he never can come into the world
  That I live in, in my thought.

For whether I wake, or whether I sleep,
   It is always just the same ;
I am far away to the time that was,
   Or the time that never came.

Sometimes I walk in the paradise,
   That, alas ! was not to be ;
Sometimes I sit the whole night long
   A child on my father's knee ;

And when my sweet sad fancies run
   Unheeded as they list,
They go and search about to find
   The things my life has missed.

Aye ! this love is a tyrant always,
   And whether for evil or good,
Neither comes nor goes for our bidding, —
   But l've done the best I could.

And Edgar's a worthy man I know,
   And I know my house is fine ;
But I never shall live in it, mother,
   And never shall make it mine !

THE FICKLE DAY.

Last night, when the sweet young moon shone clear
   In her hall of starry splendor,
I said what a maiden loves to hear,
   To a maiden true and tender.

She promised to walk with me at noon,
    In the meadow red with clover ;
And I set her words to a pleasant tune,
    And sang them over and over.
So awake in the early dawn I lay,
    And heard the stir and humming
The glad earth makes when her orchestra
    Of a thousand birds is coming.

I saw the waning lights in the skies
    Blown out by the breath of morning ;
And the morn grow pale as a maid who dies,
    When her loving wins but scorning.
And I said, The day will never rise ;
    On her cloudy couch she lingers,
Still pressing the lids of her sweet blue eyes
    Close shut with her rosy fingers.
But she rose at last, and stood arrayed
    Like a queen for a royal crowning,
And I thought her look was never made
    For changing or for frowning.

But alas for the dreams that round us play !
    For the plans of mortal making !
And alas for the false and fickle day
    That looked so fair at waking !
For suddenly on the world she frowned,
    Till the birds grew still in their places,
And the blossoms turned their eyes on the ground
    To hide their frightened faces.
And the light grew checkered where it lay,
    Across the hill and meadow,
For she hid her sunny hair away
    Under a net of shadow.

And close in the folds of a cloudy veil,
    Her altered beauty keeping,
She breathed a low and lonesome wail,
    And softly fell a-weeping.
And now, my dream of the time to be,
    My beautiful dream is over;
For no maiden will walk at noon with me
    In the meadow red with clover.
And within and without I feel and see
    But woeful, weary weather;
Ah! wretched day; ah! wretched me —
    We well may weep together!

THE MAID OF KIRCONNEL.

FAIR Kirtle, hastening to the sea,
    Through banks of sunniest green,
But for thy tender witchery
" Fair Helen, of Kirconnel lea,"
    A happier fate had seen.

And wood-bower sweet, whose vines displayed
    A royal wealth of flowers;
Why did you lure the dreaming maid,
So oft beneath your haunted shade,
    To pass the charmèd hours?

For hidden, like the feathery choir,
    There from the noontide's glance,
She lit the heart's first vestal fire,
And fed its flame of soft desire,
    With dreams of old romance.

Poor, frightened doe, that sought the shade
    Of that sequestered place ;
And led the tender, timid maid,
Blushing, surprised, and half afraid,
    To meet the hunter's face.

Not thine the fault, but thine the deed,
    Blind, harmless innocent ;
When to that bosom, doomed to bleed,
With cruel, swift, unerring speed,
    The fatal arrow went.

Why came no warning voice to save,
    No cry upon the blast,
When Helen fair, and Fleming brave,
Sat on the dead Kirconnel's grave,
    And spake, and kissed their last ?

O Mary, gone in life's young bloom,
    O " Mary of the le,"
Couldst thou not leave one hour the tomb,
To save her from that hapless doom,
    So soon to sleep by thee ?

Vain, vain, to say what might have been,
    Or strive with cruel Fate ;
Evil the world hath entered in,
And sin is death, and death is sin,
    And love must trust and wait.

For here the crown of lovers true
    Still hides its flowers beneath —

The sharpest thorns that ever grew,
The thorns that pierce us through and through,
   And make us bleed to death!

SAINT MACARIUS OF THE DESERT.

Good Saint Macarius, full of grace,
   And happy as none but a saint can be,
Abode in his cell, in a desert place,
   With only angels for company;
And fasting daily till vesper time,
And praying oft till the hour of prime;
   He wept so freely for all the sin
That ever had stained his soul below,
   That, though the hue of his guilt had been
As scarlet, it must have changed to snow.

The Tempter scarce could charm his sight
Who came transformed to an angel of light;
The demons that pursued his track
He sent to a fiercer torment back;
And he wearied, with fast and penance grim,
The fiends that were sent to weary him
Until at last it came about
   That he vanquished the fiercest of Satan's brood,
And the powers of darkness, tired out,
   Had left the anchoret unsubdued.

Yet I marvel what they could have been
   The sins that he strove to wash away;
For he had fled from the haunts of men
   In the pure, sweet dawn of his manhood's day.

But surely now they were all forgiven,
    For alone in the desert, for sixty years,
He had eat of its scant herbs morn and even,
    And black bread, moistened with bitter tears.

Yet so cunning and subtle is the mesh
    For the souls of the unwary laid,
And so strong is the power of the world and flesh,
    That the very elect have been betrayed.
And therefore even our holy saint,
    When fast and penance and watch were done,
Made often bitter and loud complaint
    Of the artful wiles of the Evil One.
For he found that none may flee from his ire,
    Or find a refuge and safe retreat,
In the time when Satan doth desire
    To have and to sift the soul like wheat.

Good Saint Macarius, having passed
    The long, hot hours of the day in prayer,
Rose once an hungered, after a fast
    That was long for even a saint to bear.
And looking without, where the shadows fell —
    'Twas a sight most rare in that lonely place —
Just at the door of his humble cell
    He saw a stranger face to face,
Who greeted him in a tender tone,
    That fell on his weary heart like balm,
As graciously from out his own
    He dropped in the hermit's open palm
A cluster plucked from a fruitful vine,
Ripe and ruddy, and full of wine.

" Thanks," said the saint, for his heart was glad,
  " My blessing take for a righteous deed ;
  'Tis the very gift I would have had
    For one in his sore distress and need."

Then, seizing a staff in his eager hand,
He hurried over the burning sand,
To a cell where a holy brother lay,
Wasting and dying day by day,
And gave, his dying thirst to slake,
The fruit 'twere a sin for himself to take.

Alas ! the fainting hermit said,
To the holy brother who watched his bed,
Short at the worst can be my stay
In this vile and wretched house of clay ;
For my night is almost done below,
And at break of day I must rise and go,
Shall I yield at last the flesh to please,
And lose my soul for a moment's ease ?
Nay, take this gift to my precious son,
Whose weary journey is scarce begun,
For the burden of penance and fast and prayer
Is a heavier thing for the young to bear.
Therefore his sin were not as mine,
Though he ate the pleasant fruit of the vine.

So, before another hour had gone,
The will of the dying man was done ;
And the fair young monk, who had come to dwell
For the good of his soul in a desert-cell,
Had bound the sandals on his feet,
  And drawn his hood about his head,

16

And, bearing the cluster ripe and sweet,
   Was crossing the desert with cheerful tread.

For he said, 'Twere well that an aged saint
   Should break his fast with fruits like these ;
But I in my vigor dare not taint
   My soul with self-indulgencies.
And the holy father whom I seek,
   By praying and fasting oft and long,
I fear me makes the flesh too weak
To keep the spirit brave and strong.

At the day-break Saint Macarius rose
   From his peaceful sleep with conscience clear
And lo ! the youngest monk of those
   Who lived in a desert-cell drew near ;
And, greeting his father in the Lord,
   Passed reverently the open door.
And again the hermit had on his board
   The fruit untouched as it was before.

Then Saint Macarius joyful raised
   His thankful eyes and hands to heaven,
And cried aloud : " The saints be praised
   That unto all my sons was given
Such strength that, tempted as they have been,
Not a single soul hath yielded to sin."

And then, though he had not broken fast,
   The lure was firmly put aside ;
And in the future, as in the past,
A self-denying man to the last,
   Good Saint Macarius lived and died.

And he never tasted the fruit of the vine,
   Till he went to a righteous man's reward,
And took of the heavenly bread and wine
   New in the kingdom of the Lord.

FAIR ELEANOR.

WHEN the birds were mating and building
   To the sound of a pleasant tune,
Fair Eleanor sat on the porch and spun
   All the long bright afternoon.
She wound the flax on the distaff,
   She spun it fine and strong;
She sung as it slipped through her hands, and this
   Was the burden of her song:
"I sit here spinning, spinning,
   And my heart beats joyfully,
Though my lover is riding away from me
   To his home by the hills of the sea."

When the shining skeins were finished,
   And the loom its work had done,
Fair Eleanor brought her linen out
   To spread on the grass in the sun.
She sprinkled it over with water,
   She turned and bleached it white;
And still she sung, and the burden
   Was gay, as her heart was light:
"O sun, keep shining, shining!
   O web, bleach white for me!
For now my lover is riding back
   From his home by the hills of the sea."

When the sun, through the leaves of Autumn,
    Burned with a dull-red flame,
Fair Eleanor had made the robes
    To wear when her lover came.
And she stood at the open clothes-press,
    And the roses burned in her face,
As she strewed with roses and lavender
    Her folded linen and lace ;
And she murmured softly, softly :
    "My bridegroom draws near to me,
And we shall ride back together
    To his home by the hills of the sea."

When the desolate clouds of Winter
    Shrouded the face of the sun,
Then the fair, fair Eleanor, wedded,
    Was dressed in the robes she had spun.
But never again in music
    Did her silent lips dispart,
Though her lover came from his home by the sea,
    And clasped her to his heart ;
Though he cried, as he kissed and kissed her,
    Till his sobs through the house were heard —
Ah, she was too happy where she had gone,
    I ween to answer a word !

BREAKING THE ROADS.

ABOUT the cottage, cold and white,
    The snow-drifts heap the ground ;
Through its curtains closely drawn to-night
    There scarcely steals a sound.

The task is done that patient hands
   Through all the day have plied ;
And the flax-wheel, with its loosened bands,
   Is idly set aside.

Above the hearth-fire's pleasant glare,
   Sings now the streaming spout ;
The housewife, at her evening care,
   Is passing in and out.

And still as here and there she flits,
   With cheerful, bustling sound,
Musing, her daughter silent sits,
   With eyes upon the ground.

A maiden, womanly and true,
   Sweet as the mountain-rose ;
No fairer form than hers ere grew
   Amid the winter snows.

A rosy mouth, and o'er her brow
   Brown, smoothly-braided hair,
Surely the youth beside her now
   Must covet flower so fair.

For bashfulness she dare not meet
   His eyes that keep their place,
So steadfastly and long in sweet
   Perusal of her face.

Herself is Lucy's only charm,
   To make her prized or sought ;
And Ralph hath but the goodly- farm
   Whereon his fathers wrought.

He, with his neighbors, toiling slow
   To-day till sunset's gleam,
Breaking a road-track through the snow,
   Has urged his patient team.

They came at morn from every home,
   They have labored cheerily;
They have cut a way through the snowy foam,
   As a good ship cuts the sea.

And when his tired friends were gone,
   Their pleasant labors o'er,
Ralph stayed to make a path, alone,
   To Lucy's cottage-door.

The thankful dame her friend must press
   To share her hearth's warm blaze:
What could the daughter give him less
   Than words of grateful praise?

And now the board has given its cheer,
   The eve has nearly gone,
Yet by the hearth-fire bright and clear
   The youth still lingers on.

The mother rouses from her nap,
   Her task awhile she keeps;
At last, with knitting on her lap,
   Tired nature calmly sleeps.

Then Lucy, bringing from the shelf
   Apples that mock her cheeks,
Falls working busily herself,
   And half in whisper speaks.

And Ralph, for very bashfulness,
    Is held a moment mute ;
Then drawing near, he takes in his
    The hand that pares the fruit.

Then Lucy strives to draw away
    Her hand, yet kindly too,
And half in his she lets it stay, —
    She knows not what to do.

" Darling," he cries, with flushing cheek,
    " Forego awhile your task ;
Lift up your downcast eyes and speak,
    'Tis but a word I ask ! "

He sees the color rise and wane
    Upon the maiden's face ;
Then with a kiss he sets again
    The red rose in its place.

The mother wakes in strange surprise,
    And wondering looks about, —
" How careless, Lucy dear," she cries ;
    " You've let the fire go out ! "

Then Lucy turned her face away,
    She did not even speak ;
But she looked as if the live coals lay
    A-burning in her cheek.

" Ralph," said the dame, " you ne'er before
    Played such a double part :
Have you made the way both to my door
    . And to my daughter's heart ? "

" I've tried my best," cried happy Ralph,
　" And if she'll be my wife,
I'll make a pathway smooth and safe
　For my darling all her life ! "

All winter from his home to that
　Where Lucy lived content,
Along a path made hard and straight,
　Her lover came and went.

And when Spring smiled in all her bowers,
　And birds sang far and wide,
He trod a pathway through the flowers,
　And led her home a bride !

PERSONAL POEMS.

READY.

Loaded with gallant soldiers,
  A boat shot in to the land,
And lay at the right of Rodman's Point,
  With her keel upon the sand.

Lightly, gayly, they came to shore,
  And never a man afraid,
When sudden the enemy opened fire,
  From his deadly ambuscade.

Each man fell flat on the bottom
  Of the boat; and the captain said:
" If we lie here, we all are captured,
  And the first who moves is dead! "

Then out spoke a negro sailor,
  No slavish soul had he;
" Somebody's got to die, boys,
  And it might as well be me! "

Firmly he rose, and fearlessly
  Stepped ont into the tide;
He pushed the vessel safely off,
  Then fell across her side:

Fell, pierced by a dozen bullets,
    As the boat swung clear and free ; —
But there wasn't a man of them that day
    Who was fitter to die than he !

DICKENS.

"One story more," the whole world cried.
    The great magician smiled in doubt:
"I am so tired that, if I tried,
    I fear I could not tell it out."

"But one is all we ask," they said ;
    "You surely cannot faint nor fail." .
Again he raised his weary head,
    And slow began the witching tale.

The fierce debater's tongue grew mute,
    Wise men were silent for his sake ;
The poet threw aside his lute,
    And paused enraptured while he spake.

The proudest lady in the land
    Forgot that praise and power were sweet ;
She dropped the jewels from her hand,
    And sat enchanted at his feet.

Lovers, with clasped hands lightly prest,
    Saw Hope's sweet blossoms bud and bloom ;
Men, hastening to their final rest,
    Stopped, half-enraptured with the tomb.

Children, with locks of brown and gold,
  Gathered about like flocks of birds;
The poor, whose story he had told,
  Drew near and loved him for his words.

His eye burns bright, hisvoice is strong,
  A waiting people eager stands;
Men on the outskirts of the throng
  Interpret him to distant lands.

When lo! his accents, faltering, fall;
  The nations, awe-struck, hold their breath;
The great magician, loved of all,
  Has sunk to slumber, tired to death!

His human eyes in blind eclipse
  Are from the world forever sealed;
The "mystery" trembling on his lips
  Shall never, never be revealed.

Yet who would miss that tale half told,
  Though weird and strange, or sweet and true;
Who care to listen to the old,
  If he could hear the strange and new?

Alas! alas! it cannot be;
  We too must sleep and change and rise,
To learn the eternal mystery
  That dawned upon his waking eyes!

THADDEUS STEVENS.

An eye with the piercing eagle's fire,
  Not the look of the gentle dove ;
Not his the form that men admire,
  Nor the face that tender women love.

Working first for his daily bread
  With the humblest toilers of the earth ;
Never walking with free, proud tread —
  Crippled and halting from his birth.

Wearing outside a thorny suit
  Of sharp, sarcastic, stinging power ;
Sweet at the core as sweetest fruit,
  Or inmost heart of fragrant flower.

Fierce and trenchant, the haughty foe
  Felt his words like a sword of flame ;
But to the humble, poor, and low
  Soft as a woman's his accents came.

Not his the closest, tenderest friend —
  No children blessed his lonely way ;
But down in his heart until the end
  The tender dream of his boyhood lay.

His mother's faith he held not fast ;
  But he loved her living, mourned her dead,
And he kept her memory to the last
  As green as the sod above her bed.

He held as sacred in his home
　Whatever things she wrought or planned,
And never suffered change to come
　To the work of her " industrious hand."

For her who pillowed first his head
　He heaped with a wealth of flowers the grave,
While he chose to sleep in an unmarked bed,
　By his Master's humblest poor — the slave.[1]

Suppose he swerved from the straightest course —
　That the things he should not do he did —
That he hid from the eyes of mortals, close,
　Such sins as you and I have hid?

Or suppose him worse than you ; what then ?
　Judge not, lest you be judged for sin !
One said who knew the hearts of men :
　Who loveth much shall a pardon win.

The Prince of Glory for sinners bled ;
　His soul was bought with a royal price ;
And his beautified feet on flowers may tread
　To-day with his Lord in Paradise.

---

[1] Thaddeus Stevens, who cared nothing about his own burial-place, except that the spot should be one from which the humblest of his fellow-creatures were not excluded, left by will one thousand dollars to beautify and adorn the grave of his mother

RELIGIOUS POEMS.

THE WIDOW'S THANKSGIVING.

Of the precious years of my life, to-day
    I count another one ;
And I thank thee, Lord, for the light is good,
    And 'tis sweet to see the sun.

To watch the seasons as they pass,
    Their wondrous wealth unfold,
Till the silvery treasures of the snow
    Are changed to the harvest's gold.

For kindly still does the teeming earth
    Her stores of plenty yield,
Whether we come to bind the sheaves,
    Or only to glean in the field.

And dwelling in such a pleasant land,
    Though poor in goods and friends,
We may still be rich, if we live content
    With what our Father sends.

If we feel that life is a blessed thing —
    A boon to be desired ;
And where not much to us is given,
    Not much will be required ;

And keep our natures sweet with the sense
   Of fervent gratitude,
That we have been left to live in the world,
   And to know that God is good!

And since there is naught of all we have,
   That we have not received:
Shall we dare, though our treasures be reclaimed,
   To call ourselves bereaved?

For 'tis easy to walk by sight in the day;
   'Tis the night that tries our faith;
And what is that worth if we render thanks
   For life and not for death?

Lo! I glean alone! and the children, Lord,
   Thou gavest unto me,
Have one by one fled out of my arms,
   And into eternity.

Aye, the last and the bravest of them died
   In prison, far away;
And no man, of his sepulchre,
   Knoweth the place to-day.

Yet is not mine the bitterness
   Of the soul that doth repent;
If I had it now to do again,
   I would bless him that he went.

There are many writ in the book of life
   Whose graves are marked unknown;
For his country and his God he died,
   And He will know his own!

In the ranks he fought; but he stood the first
   And bravest in the lines;
And no fairer, brighter name than his
   On the roll of honor shines.

And because he faltered not, nor failed
   In the march, nor under fire;
His great promotion came at last,
   In the call to go up higher.

Fair wives, whose homes are guarded round
   By love's securities;
Mothers, who gather all your flock
   At night about your knees;

Thrice happy, happy girls, who hold
   The hand of your lovers fast;
Widows, who keep an only son.
   To be your stay to the last:

You never felt, though you give God thanks
   For his blessings day by day.
That perfect peace which blesses Him
   For the good He takes away;

The joy of a soul that even in pain
   Beholds his love's decrees,
Who sets the solitary ones
   'n the midst of famil'e .

Lord, help me still, at the midnight hour,
   My lamp of faith to trim;
And to sing from my heart, at the break of day.
   A glad thanksgiving hymn:

Nor doubt thy love, though my earthly joys
    Were narrowed down to this one,
So long as the sweet day shines for me,
    And mine eyes behold the sun.

VIA CRUCIS, VIA LUCIS.

QUESTIONING, blind, unsatisfied,
Out of the dark my spirit cried, —
Wherefore for sinners, lost, undone,
Gave the Father his only Son ?

Clear and sweet there came reply, —
Out of my soul or out of the sky
A voice like music answered : —
God so loved the world, it said.

Could not the Lord from heaven give aid ?
Why was He born of the mother-maid?
Only the Son of man could be
Touched with man's infirmity !

Why must He lay his infant head
In the manger, where the beasts were fed :
So that the poorest here might cry,
My Lord was as lowly born as I !

Why for friends did He choose to know
Sinners and harlots here below ?
Not to the righteous did He come,
But to find and bring the wanderers home

17

He was tempted?   *Yes, He sounded then*
All that hides in the hearts of men ;
And He knoweth, when we intercede,
How to succor our souls in their need.

Why should they whom He called his own,
Deny, hetray Him, leave Him alone?
That He might know their direst pain,
Who have trusted human love in vain !

Must He needs have washed the traitor's feet
Ere his abasement was made complete?
Yea, for women have thus laid down
Their hearts for a Judas to trample on !

By one cup might He not drink less ;
Nor lose one drop of the bitterness ;
Must He suffer, though without blame,
Stripes and buffeting, scorn and shame ?

Alas ! and wherefore should it he
That He must die on Calvary ;
Must bear the pain and the cruel thrust,
Till his heart with its very anguish burst?

That martyrs, dying for his name,
Whether by cross, or flood, or flame,
Might know they were called to bear no more
Than He, their blessed Master, bore.

What did He feel in that last dread cry ?
The height and the depth of agony !
All the anguish a mortal can,
Who dies forsaken of God and man !

Is there no way to Him at last
But that where His bleeding feet have passed?
Did He not to his followers say,
I am the Life, the Light, the Way?

Yea, and still from the heavens He saith
The gate of life is the gate of death;
Peace is the crown of faith's good fight,
And the way of the cross is the way of light!

HYMN.

COME down, O Lord, and with us live!
  For here with tender, earnest call,
The gospel thou didst freely give,
  We freely offer unto all.

Come, with such power and saving grace,
  That we shall cry, with one accord,
" How sweet and awful is this place, —
  This sacred temple of the Lord."

Let friend and stranger, one in·thee,
  Feel with such power thy Spirit move,
That every man's own speech shall be,
  The sweet eternal speech of love.

Yea, fill us with the Holy Ghost,
  Let burning hearts and tongues be given,
Make this a day of Pentecost,
  A foretaste of the bliss of heaven!

OF ONE FLESH.

A MAN he was who loved the good,
　　Yet strayed in crooked ways apart;
He could not do the thing he would,
　　Because of evil in his heart.

He saw men garner wealth and fame,
　　Ripe in due time, a precious load;
He fainted ere the harvest came,
　　And failed to gather what he sowed.

He looked if haply grapes had grown
　　On the wild thorns that choked his vines;
When clear the truth before him shone
　　He sought for wonders and for signs.

Others Faith's sheltered harbor found,
　　The while his bark was tossed about;
Drifting and dragging anchor round
　　The troubled, shoreless sea of doubt.

Where he would win, he could not choose
　　But yield to weakness and despair;
He ran as they who fear to lose,
　　And fought as one who beats the air.

Walking where hosts of souls have passed,
　　By faith and hope made strong and brave,
He, groping, stumbled at the last,
　　And blindly fell across the grave.

Yet speak of him in charity,
  O man ! nor write of blame one line ;
Say that thou wert not such as he —
  He was thy brother, and was mine !

TEACH US TO WAIT !

WHY are we so impatient of delay,
  Longing forever for the time to be ?
For thus we live to-morrow in to-day,
  Yea, sad to-morrows we may never see.

We are too hasty ; are not reconciled
  To let kind Nature do her work alone :
We plant our seed, and like a foolish child
  We dig it up to see if it has grown.

The good that is to be we covet now,
  We cannot wait for the appointed hour ;
Before the fruit is ripe, we shake the bough,
  And seize the bud that folds away the flower.

When midnight darkness reigns we do not see
  That the sad night is mother of the morn ;
We cannot think our own sharp agony,
  May be the birth-pang of a joy unborn.

Into the dust we see our idols cast,
  · And cry, that death has triumphed, life is void !
We do not trust the promise, that the last
  Of all our enemies shall be destroyed !

With rest almost in sight the spirit faints,
   And heart and flesh grow weary at the last;
Our feet would walk the city of the saints,
   Even before the silent gate is passed.

Teach us to wait until thou shalt appear—
   To know that all thy ways and times are just;
Thou seest that we do believe, and fear,
   Lord, make us also to believe and trust !

IN HIS ARMS.

IF when thy children, O my friend,
   Were clasped by thee, in love's embrace,
Their guardian angels, that in heaven,
   Always behold the Father's face;

Thine earthly home, on shining wings,
   Had entered, as of old they came,
To grant to these whatever good,
   Thou shouldst desire, in Jesus' name; —

Or as the loving sinner came,
   And worshipped when He sat at meat,
Couldst thou, thyself have come to Him,
   And bowed thy forehead to his feet;

And prayed Him by that tender love,
   He feels for those to whom He came,   ·
To give to thy beloved ones,
   The best thou couldst desire or name; —

What couldst thou ask so great as this,
   Out of his love's rich treasury,
That He should take them in his arms,
   And bless, and keep them safe for thee?

Ah! favored friend, nor faith, nor prayers,
   Nor richest offering ever brought
A token of the Saviour's love
   So sweet, as thou hast gained unsought!

———

THE heart is not satisfied :
For more than the world can give it pleads;
It has infinite wants and infinite needs;
And its every beat is an awful cry
For love that never can change nor die ;
   The heart is not satisfied !

UNBELIEF.

FAITHLESS, perverse, and blind,
   We sit in our house of fear,
When the winter of sorrow comes to our souls,
   And the days of our life are drear.

For when in darkness and clouds
   The way of God is concealed,
We doubt the words of his promises,
   And the glory to be revealed.

We do but trust in part;
   We grope in the dark alone ;

Lord, when shall we see thee as thou art,
  And know as we are known?

When shall we live to thee
  And die to thee, resigned,
Nor fear to hide what we would keep,
  And lose what we would find?

For we doubt our Father's care,
  We cover our faces and cry,
If a little cloud, like the hand of a man,
  Darkens the face of our sky.

We judge of his perfect day
  By our life's poor glimmering spark:
And measure eternity's circle
  By the segment of an arc.

We say, they have taken our Lord,
  And we know not where He lies,
When the light of his resurrection morn
  Is breaking out of the skies.

And we stumble at last when we come
  On the brink of the grave to stand;
As if the souls that are born of his love
  Could slip their Father's hand?

THE VISION ON THE MOUNT.

OH, if this living soul, that many a time
Above the low things of the earth doth climb,
Up to the mountain-top of faith sublime,

If she could only stay
In that high place alway,
And hear, in reverence bowed,
God's voice behind the cloud:

Or if descending to the earth again
Its lesson in the heart might still remain;
If we could keep the vision, clear and plain,
  Nor let one jot escape,
  So that we still might shape
  Our lives to deeds sublime
  By that exalted time:

Ah! what a world were ours to journey through!
What deeds of love and mercy we should do:
Making our lives so beautiful and true,
  That in our face would shine
  The light of love divine,
  Showing that we had stood
  Upon the mount of God.

But earthy of the earth, we downward tend,
From the pure height of faith our feet descend,
The hour of exaltation hath its end.
  And we, alas! forget,
  In life's turmoil and fret,
  The pattern to us shown,
  When on the mount alone.

Yea, we forget the rapture we had known,
Forget the voice that talked to us alone,
Forget the brightness past, the cloud that shone;
  We have no need to veil
  Our faces, dim and pale,

So soon from out'them dies
The sweet light of the skies.

We come down from the height where we have been,
And build our tabernacles low and mean,
Not by the pattern in the vision seen
    Remembering no more,
    When once the hour is o'er,
How in the safe cleft of the rock on high,
The shadow of the Lord has passed us by.

A CANTICLE.

BE with me, O Lord, when my life hath increase
    Of the riches that make it complete ;
When, favored, I walk in the pathway of peace,
    That is pleasant and safe to the feet:
Be with me and keep me, when all the day long
    Delight hath no taint of alloy ;
When my heart runneth over with laughter and song,
    And my cup with the fullness of joy.

Be with me, O Lord, when I make my complaint
    Because of my sorrow and care ;
Take the weight from my soul, that is ready to faint,
    And give me thy burden to bear.
If the sun of the desert at noontide, in wrath
    Descends on my shelterless head,
Be thou the cool shadow and rock in the path
    Of a land that is weary to tread.

In the season of sorest affliction and dread,
   When my soul is encompassed with fears,
Till I lie in the darkness awake on my bed,
   And water my pillow with tears ;
When lonely and sick, for the tender delight
   Of thy comforting presence I pray,
Come into my chamber, O Lord, in the night,
   And stay till the break of the day.

Through the devious paths of the world be my guide,
   Till its trials, and its dangers are past ;
If I walk through the furnace, be thou by my side,
   Be my rod and my staff to the last.
When my cruelest enemy presses me hard
   To my last earthly refuge and rest —
Put thy arms underneath and about me, O Lord,
   Let me lie tenderly on thy breast.

Come down when in silence I slumber alone,
   When the death seal is set on mine eyes ;
Break open the sepulchre, roll off the stone,
   And bear me away to the skies.
Lord, lay me to rest by the river, that bright
   From the throne of thy glory doth flow ;
Where the odorous beds of the lilies are white
   And the roses of paradise blow !

THE CRY OF THE HEART AND FLESH.

WHEN her mind was sore bewildered,
   And her feet were gone astray,
When she saw no fiery column,
   And no cloud before her way, —

Then, with earnest supplication,
　To the mighty One she prayed,
" Thou for whom we were created,
　And by whom the worlds were made, —
By thy pity for our weakness,
　By thy wisdom and thy might,
Son of God, Divine Redeemer!
　Guide and keep me in the right!"

When Faith had broke her moorings,
　And upon a sea of doubt,
Her soul with fear and darkness
　Was encompassed round about;
Then she said, " O Elder Brother!
　By thy human nature, when
Thou wert made to be in all things
　Like unto the sons of men;
By the hour of thy temptation,
　By thy one forsaken cry,
Son of God and man! have mercy,
　Send thy light down from on high!'

When her very heart was broken,
　Bearing more than it could bear,
Then she clasped her anguish, crying,
　In her passionate despair, —
" Thou who wert beloved of women,
　And who gav'st them love again,
By the strength of thine affection,
　By its rapture and its pain,
Son of God and Son of woman!
　Lo! 'tis now the eventide!

Come from heaven, O sacred lover!
   With thine handmaid to abide ;
Come down as the bridegroom cometh
   From his chamber to the bride ! "

OUR PATTERN.

A WEAVER sat one day at his loom,
   Among the colors bright,
With the pattern for his copying
   Hung fair and plain in sight.

But the weaver's thoughts were wandering
   Away on a distant track,
As he threw the shuttle in his hand
   Wearily forward and back.

And he turned his dim eyes to the ground,
   And tears fell on the woof,
. For his thoughts, alas ! were not with his home,
   Nor the wife beneath its roof ;

When her voice recalled him suddenly
   To himself, as she sadly said :
" Ah ! woe is me ! for your work is spoiled,
   And what will we do for bread ? "

And then the weaver looked, and saw
   His work must be undone ;
For the threads were wrong, and the colors dimmed,
   Where the bitter tears had run.

"Alack, alack!" said the weaver,
  "And this had all been right
If I had not looked at my work, but kept
    The pattern in my sight!"

Ah! sad it was for the weaver,
  And sad for his luckless wife;
And sad will it be for us, if we say,
  At the end of our task of life:

"The colors that we had to weave
    Were bright in our early years;
But we wove the tissue wrong, and stained
    The woof with bitter tears.

"We wove a web of doubt and fear —
    Not faith, and hope, and love —
Because we looked at our work, and not
    At our Pattern up above!"

THE EARTHLY HOUSE.

"Ye are the temple of God. . . . . If any man defile the temple of God, him will God destroy; for the temple of God is holy." — 1 Co-RINTHIANS iii. 16, 17.

ONCE — in the ages that have passed away,
Since the fair morning of that fairest day,
When earth, in all her innocent beauty, stood
Near her Creator, and He called her good —
He who had weighed the planets in his hand,
And dropped them in the places where they stand,

Builded a little temple white and fair,
And of a workmanship so fine and rare
Even the star that led to Bethlehem
Had not the value of this wondrous gem.

Then, that its strength and beauty might endure,
He placed within, to keep it clean and pure,
A living human soul.   To him He said :
" This is the temple which my hands have made
To be thy dwelling place, or foul or fair,
As thou shalt make it by neglect or care.
Mar or deface this temple's sacred wall,
And swift destruction on the work shall fall ;
Preserve it perfect in its purity,
And God Himself shall come and dwell with thee ! "

Then he for whom that holy place was built,
Fair as a palace — ah, what fearful guilt ! —
Grew, after tending it a little while,
Careless, then reckless, and then wholly vile.
The evil spirits came and dwelt with him ;
The walls decayed, and through the windows dim
He saw not this world's beauty any more,
Heard no good angel knocking at his door ;
And all his house, because of sin and crime,
Tumbled and fell in ruin ere its time.

Oh, men and brethren ! we who live to-day
In dwellings made by God, though made of clay,
Have these our mortal bodies ever been
Kept fit for Him who made them pure and clean ;
Or was that soul in evil sunk so deep,
He spoiled the temple he was set to keep,

And turned to wastefulness and to abuse
The tastes and passions that were meant for use ;
So like ourselves, that we, afraid, might cry :
" Lord, who destroyest the temple — is it I ? "

YE DID IT UNTO ME.

SINNER, careless, proud, and cold,
Straying from the sheltering fold,
Hast thou thought how patiently
The Good Shepherd follows thee ;
Still with tireless, toiling feet,
Through the tempest and the heat —
Thought upon that yearning breast,
Where He fain would have thee rest,
And of all its tender pain,
While He seeks for thee in vain ?

Dost thou know what He must feel,
Making vainly his appeal ;
When He knocketh at thy door
Present entrance to implore ;
Saying, " *Open unto Me,*
I will come and sup with thee " —
Forced to turn away at last
From the portal shut and fast ?
Wilt thou careless slumber on,
Even till thy Lord has gone,
Heedless of his high behest,
His desire to be thy guest ?

Sinner, sinner, dost thou know
What it is to slight Him so?
Sitting careless by the sea
While He calleth, " *Follow me* " ;
Sleeping, thoughtless, unaware
Of his agonizing prayer,
While thy sins his soul o'erpower,
And thou canst not watch one hour?
Our infirmities He bore,
And our mortal form He wore ;
Yea, our Lord was made to be
Here in all things like as we,
And, that pardon we might win,
He, the sinless, bare our sin !

Sinner, though He comes no more
Faint and fasting to thy door,
His disciples here instead
Thou canst give the cup and bread.
If his lambs thou dost not feed,
He it is that feels their need ;
He that suffers their distress,
Hunger, thirst, and weariness ;
He that loving them again
Beareth all their bitter pain !
Canst thou then so reckless prove,
Canst thou, darest thou slight his love ?

Do not, sinner, for thy sake
Make Him still the cross to take,
And ascend again for thee
Dark and dreadful Calvary !
18

Do not set the crown of pain
On that sacred head again ;
Open all afresh and wide
Closèd wounds in hands and side.
Do not, do not scorn his name,
Putting Him to open shame !

Oh, by all the love He knew
For his followers, dear and true ;
By the sacred tears He wept
At the tomb where Lazarus slept;
By Gethsemane's bitter cry,
That the cup might pass Him by ;
By that wail of agony,
Why hast thou forsaken me ?
By that last and heaviest stroke,
When his heart for sinners broke,
Do not let Him lose the price
Of his awful sacrifice !

THE SINNER AT THE CROSS.

HELPLESS before the cross I lay,
  With all to lose, or all to win,
My steps had wandered from the way,
  My soul was burdened with her sin ;
I spoke no word, I made no plea,
But this, *Be merciful to me !*

To meet his gaze, I could not brook,
  Who for my sake ascended there ;

I could not bear the angry look
  My dear offended Lord must wear ;
Remembering how I had denied
His name, my heart within me died.

Almost I heard his awful voice,
  Sounding above my head in wrath ;
Fixing my everlasting choice,
  With such as tread the downward path ;
I waited for the words, *Depart*
From me, accursed as thou art !

One moment, all the world was stilled,
  Then, He who saw my anguish, spoke ;
I heard, I breathed, my pulses thrilled,
  And heart, and brain, and soul, awoke ;
No scorn, no wrath, was in that tone,
But pitying love, and love alone !

" And dost thou know, and love not me,"
  He said, " when I have loved thee so ;
It was for guilty men like thee
  I came into this world of woe ;
To save the lost I lived and died,
For sinners was I crucified."

The fountain of my tears was dried,
  My eyes were lifted from the dust :
" Jesus ! my blessed Lord ! I cried,
  And is it thou, I feared to trust ?
And art thou He, I deemed my foe ;
The Friend to whom I dared not go ?

" How could I shrink from such as thou,
  Divine Redeemer, as thou art !
I know thy loving kindness now,
  I see thy wounded, bleeding heart ;
I know that thou didst give me thine,
And all that thou dost ask, is mine !

" My Lord, my God ! I know at last
  Whose mercy I have dared offend ;
I own thee now, I hold thee fast,
  My Brother, Lover, and my Friend !
Take me and clasp me to thy breast,
Bless me again, and keep me blest !

" Thou art the man, who ne'er refused
  With sinful men to sit at meat ;
Who spake to her who was accused
  Of men, and trembling at thy feet,
As lips had never spoke before,
Go uncondemned, and sin no more.

" Dear Lord ! not all eternity
  Thy image from my heart can move,
When thou didst turn and look on me,
  When first I heard thy words of love ;
Repent, believe, and thou shalt be,
To-night in Paradise with me."

THE HEIR.

An orphan, through the world
    Unfriended did I roam,
I knew not that my Father lived,
    Nor that I had a home.

No kindred might I claim,
    No lover sought for me ;
Mine was a solitary life,
    Set in no family.

I yielded to despair,
    I sorrowed night and morn —
I cried, " Ah ! good it were for me,
    If I had not been born ! " •

At midnight came a man —
    He knocked upon my door ;
He spake such tender words as man
    Ne'er spake to me before.

I rose to let him in,
    I shook with fear and dread ;
A lamp was shining in his hand,
    A brightness round his head.

'" And who art thou," I cried ;
    " I scarce for awe might speak ;
And why for such a wretch as I
    Dost thou at midnight seek ? "

"Though thou hast strayed," He said,
  " From me thou couldst not flee ;
I am thy Brother and thy Friend,
  And thou shalt share with me !

" For me thou hast not sought,
  I sought thee everywhere ;
Thou hast a Father and a home,
  With mansions grand and fair.

" To thine inheritance
  I came thy soul to bring ;
Thou art the royal heir of heaven —
  The daughter of the King ! "

REALITIES.

THINGS that I have to hold and keep, ah ! these
  Are not the treasures to my heart most dear ;
Though many sweet and precious promises
  Have had their sweet fulfillment, even here.

And yet to others, what I name my own
  Poor unrealities and shows might seem ;
Since my best house hath no foundation-stone,
  My tenderest lover is a tender dream.

And would you learn who leads me, if below
  I choose the good or from the ill forbear?
A little child *He* suffered long ago
  To come unto his arms, and keeps her there !

The alms I *give* the beggar at my gate　.
　I do but *lend* to One who thrice repays;
The only heavenly bread I ever ate
　Came back to find me, after many days.

The single friend whose presence cannot fail,
　Whose face I always see without disguise,
Went down into the grave and left the veil
　Of mortal flesh that hid her from my eyes !

My clearest way is that which faith hath shown,
　Not that in which by sight I daily move ;
And the most precious thing my soul hath known
　Is that which passeth knowledge, God's dear love.

HYMN.

When the world no solace gives,
　When in deep distress I groan ;
When my lover and my friend
　Leave me with my grief alone ;
When a weary land I tread,
　Fainting for the rocks and springs,
Overshadow me, O Lord,
　With the comfort of thy wings !

When my heart and flesh shall fail,
　When I yield my mortal breath,
When I gather up my feet,
　Icy with the chill of death ;

Strengthen and sustain me, Lord,
　With thine all-sufficient grace :
Overlean my dying bed
　With the sweetness of thy face !

When the pang, the strife is past,
　When my spirit mounts on high,
Catch me up in thine embrace,
　In thy bosom let me lie !
Freed from sin and freed from death,
　Hid with thee, in heaven above,
Oversplendor me, O God,
　With the glory of thy love.

WOUNDED.

O MEN, with wounded souls,
　O women, with broken hearts,
That have suffered since ever the world was made,
　And nobly borne your parts ;

Suffered and borne as well
　As the martyrs whom we name,
That went rejoicing home, through flood,
　Or singing through the flame ;

Ye have had of Him reward
　For your battles fought and won,
Who giveth his beloved rest
　When the day of their work is done.

Ye have changed for perfect peace
The pain of the ways ye trod;
And laid your burdens softly down,
At the merciful feet of God!

A CRY OF THE HEART.

Oh, for a mind more clear to see,
A hand to work more earnestly
　　For every good intent;
Oh, for a Peter's fiery zeal,
His conscience always quick to feel,
　　And instant to repent!

Oh, for a faith more strong and true
Than that which doubting Thomas knew,
　　A faith assured and clear;
To know that He who for us died,
Rejected, scorned, and crucified,
　　Lives, and is with us here

Oh, for the blessing shed upon
That humble, loving, sinful one,
　　Who, when He sat at meat,
With precious store of ointment came;
Hid from her Lord her face for shame,
　　And laid it on his feet.

Oh, for that look of pity seen
By her, the guilty Magdalene,
　　Who stood her Judge before;
And listening, for her comfort heard,
The tender, sweet, forgiving word: —
　　Go thou, and sin no more!

Oh, to have stood with James and John,
Where brightness round the Saviour shone,
    Whiter than light of day ;
When by the voice and cloud dismayed,
They fell upon the ground afraid,
    And wist not what to say.

Oh, to have been the favored guest,
That leaned at supper on his breast,
    And heard his dear Lord say :
He who shall testify of Me,
The Comforter, ye may not see
    Except I go away.

Oh, for the honor won by her,
Who early to the sepulchre
    Hastened in tearful gloom ;
To whom He gave his high behest,
To tell to Peter and the rest,
    Their Lord had left the tomb.

Oh, for the vision that sufficed
That first blest martyr after Christ,
    And gave a peace so deep,
That while he saw with raptured eyes
Jesus with God in Paradise,
    He, praying, fell asleep.

But if such heights I may not gain,
Oh, thou, to whom no soul in vain
    Or cries, or makes complaints ;
This only favor grant to me, —
That I of sinners chief. may be
    The least of all thy saints !

LOVE POEMS.

ON THE RIVER.

Darling, while the tender moon
Of this soft, delicious June,
Watches o'er thee like a lover;
While we journey to the sea,
Silently,
Let me tell my story over.

Ah! how clear before my sight
Rises up that summer night,
When I told thee first my passion;
And the little crimson streak,
In thy cheek,
Showed thy love in comeliest fashion.

When I pleaded for reply,
Silent lip and downcast eye,
Turning from me both dissembled;
But the lily hand that shone
In mine own,
Like a lily softly trembled.

And the pretty words that passed
O'er thy coral lips at last,
Still as precious pearls I treasure ;
And the payment lovers give,
While I live,
Shall be given thee without measure.

For I may not offer thee
Such poor words as mine must be ;
I perforce must speak my blisses
In the language of mine eyes,
Mixed with sighs,
And the tender speech of kisses.

Heart, encompassed in my heart !
Hopeful, happy as thou art,
Will I keep and ne'er forsake thee ;
Yea, my love shall hold thee fast,
Till the last,
So that heaven alone can take thee !

And if sorrow ever spread
Threatening shadows o'er thy head,
All about thee will I gather,
Whatsoever things are bright,
That thy sight
May be tempted earthward rather ;

From thy pathway, for love's sake,
Carefully my hand will take,
Every thorn anear it growing ;
And my lamb within my arms,
Safe from harms,
Will I shield when winds are blowing.

Fairest woman, holiest saint !
If my words of praise could paint
Thee, as liberal Nature made thee ;
All who saw my picture, sweet,
Would repeat,
" He who painted, loved the lady ! "

Has the wide world anything
Thou wilt take or I may bring,
I will treat no work disdainful ;
Set me some true lover's task,
Dearest, ask
Any service, sweet or painful.

If it please thee, over me,
Practice petty tyranny,
Punish me as for misdoing,
Let me make of penitence
Sad pretense,
At thy feet for pardon suing.

Darling, all our life must be,
Thou with me, and I with thee,
Calm as this delicious weather ;
We will keep our honeymoon
Every June,
Voyaging through life together.

You and me, we used to say,
We were two but yesterday ;
We were as the sea and river ;
Now our lives have all the sweetness,
And completeness
Of two souls made one forever !

INCONSTANCY.

ALL in a dreary April day,
When the light of my sky was changed to gloom
My first love drooped and faded away,
While I sorrowed over its waning bloom.

And I buried it, saying bitterly,
As I watered its grave with a rain of tears ;
" No flower of love will bloom for me
Save this one, dead in my early years !"

But the May-time pushes the April out,
And the summer of life succeeds the May ;
And the heaviest clouds of grief and doubt,
In weeping, weep themselves away.

And ere I had ceased to mourn above
My cherished flower's untimely tomb,
Right out of the grave of that buried love
There sprang another and fairer bloom.

And I cried, " Sleep softly, my perished rose,
My pretty bud of an April hour ;
While I live in the beauty that burns and glows,
In the summer heart of my passion flower !"

LOVE CANNOT DIE.

Once, when my youth was in its flower,
I lived in an enchanted bower,
    Unvexed with fear or care,
With one who made my world so bright,
I thought no darkness and no blight
    Could ever enter there.

I have no friend like that to-day,
The very bower has passed away ; ˉ
    It was not what it seemed ;
I know in all the world of men
There is not and there ne'er has been,
    That one of whom I dreamed !

And one I loved and called my friend,
And hoped to walk with to the end,·
    And on the better shore,
Has changed so cruelly that she,
Out of my years that are to be,
    Is lost for evermore.

With his dear eyes in death shut fast,
Sleeps one who loved me to the last,
    Beneath the churchyard stone ;
Yet hath his spirit always been
Near me to cheer the world wherein
    I seem to walk alone.

There was a little golden head
A few brief seasons pillowèd
    Softly my own beside ;

That pillow long has been unprest —
That child yet sleeps upon my breast
    As though she had not died,

And seeing that I always hold
Mine earthly loves, in love's sweet fold,
    I thus have learned to know,
That He, whose tenderness divine
Surpasses every thought of mine,
    Will never let me go.

Yea, thou, whose love, so strong, so great,
Nor life nor death can separate
    From souls within thy care;
I know that though in heaven I dwell,
Or go to make my bed in hell,
    Thou still art with me there !

HELPLESS.

You never said a word to me
    That was cruel, under the sun ;
It isn't the things you do, darling,
    But the things you leave undone.

If you could but know a wish or want
    You would grant it joyfully ;
Ah ! that is the worst of all, darling,
    That you cannot know nor see.

For favors free alone are sweet,
　　Not those that we must seek ;
If you loved as I love you, darling,
　　I would not need to speak.

But to-day I am helpless as a child
　　That must be led along ;
Then put your hand in mine, darling,
　　And make me brave and strong.

There's a heavy care upon my mind,
　　A trouble on my brain ;
Now gently stroke my hair, darling,
　　And take away the pain.

I feel a weight within my breast,
　　As if all had gone amiss ;
Oh, kiss me with your lips, darling,
　　And fill my heart with bliss.

Enough ! no deeper joy than this
　　For souls below is given ;
Now take me in your arms, darling,
　　And lift me up to heaven !

MY HELPER.

WE stood, my soul and I,
　　In fearful jeopardy,
The while the fire and tempest passed us by.

For I was pushed by fate
Into that fearful strait,
Where there was nothing but to stand and wait.

I had no company —
The world was dark to me :
Whence any light might come I could not see.

I lacked each common good,
Nor raiment had nor food ;
The earth seemed slipping from me where I stood.

One who had wealth essayed ;
Gold in my hand he laid ;
He proffered all his treasures for my aid.

Yet from his gilded roof,
I needs must stand aloof ;
I could not put his kindness to the proof.

One who had wisdom, said,
" By me be taught and led,
And thou, thyself, mayst win both home and bread.

Too strong and wise was he,
Too far away from me,
To help me in my great necessity.

Came one, with modest guise,
With tender, downcast eyes,
With voice as sweet as mothers' lullabies.

Softly his words did fall,
" My riches are so small
I cannot give thee anything at all.

" I cannot guide thy way,
As wiser mortals may ;
But all my true heart at thy feet I lay."

No more earth seemed to move,
The skies grew bright above ;
He gave me everything, who gave me love !

I had sweet company,
Food, raiment, luxury ;
Had all the world — had heaven come down to me !

And now such peace is mine,
Surely a light divine
Must make my face with holiest joy to shine.

So that my heart's delight
Is published in men's sight ;
And night and day I cry, and day and night ;

O soul, no more alone,
Such bliss as thine is known
But to the angels nearest love's white throne !

FAITHFUL.

Fainter and fainter may fall on my ear
The voice that is sweeter than music to hear ;
More and more eagerly then will I list,
That never a word or an accent be missed.

Slower and slower the footstep may grow,
Whose fall is the pleasantest sound that I know ;
Quicker and quicker my glad heart shall learn
To catch its faint echo and bless its return.

Whiter and whiter may turn with each day
The locks that so sadly are changing to gray ;
Dearer and dearer shall these seem to me,
The fewer and whiter and thinner they be.

Weaker and weaker may be the light clasp
Of the hand that I hold so secure in my grasp ;
Stronger and stronger my own to the last
Will cling to it, holding it tenderly fast.

Darker and darker above thee may spread
The clouds of a fate that is hopeless and dread ;
Brighter and brighter the sun of my love
Will shine, all the shadows and mists to remove.

Envy and malice thy life may assail,
Favor and fortune and friendship may fail ;
But perfect and sure, and undying shall be
The trust of this heart that is centred in thee !

POEMS OF NATURE AND HOME.

AN APRIL WELCOME.

Come up, April, through the valley,
  In your robes of beauty drest,
Come and wake your flowery children
  From their wintry beds of rest;
Come and overblow them softly
  With the sweet breath of the south;
Drop upon them, warm and loving,
  Tenderest kisses of your mouth.

Touch them with your rosy fingers,
  Wake them with your pleasant tread,
Push away the leaf-brown covers,
  Over all their faces spread;
Tell them how the sun is waiting
  Longer daily in the skies,
Looking for the bright uplifting
  Of their softly-fringèd eyes,

Call the crow-foot and the crocus,
  Call the pale anemone,.
Call the violet and the daisy,
  Clothed with careful modesty;
Seek the low and humble blossoms,
  Of their beauties unaware,
Let the dandelion and fennel,
  Show their shining yellow hair.

Bid the little homely sparrows
  Chirping, in the cold and rain,
Their impatient sweet complaining,
  Sing out from their hearts again;
Bid them set themselves to mating,
  Cooling love in softest words,
Crowd their nests, all cold and empty,
  Full of little callow birds.

Come up, April, through the valley,
  Where the fountain sleeps to-day,
Let him, freed from icy fetters,
  Go rejoicing on his way;
Through the flower-enameled meadows
  Let him run his laughing race,
Making love to all the blossoms
  That o'erlean and kiss his face.

But not birds and blossoms only,
  Not alone the streams complain,
Men and maidens too are calling,
  Come up, April, come again!
Waiting with the sweet impatience
  Of a lover for the hours
They shall set the tender beauty
  Of thy feet among the flowers!

MY NEIGHBOR'S HOUSE.

In the years that now are dead and gone —
  Aye, dead, but ne'er forgot —
My neighbor's stately house looked down
  On the walls of my humble cot.

I had my flowers and trees, 'tis true,
  But they looked not fine and tall
As my neighbor's flowers and trees, that grew
  On the other side of the wall.

Through the autumn leaves his ripe fruits gleamed
  With richer tints than mine,
And his grapes in the summer sunshine seemed
  More full of precious wine.

Through garden walk and bower I stray
  Unbidden now and free ;
For my neighbor long has passed away,
  And his wealth has come to me.

I pace those stately halls at last,
  But a darker shadow falls
Within the house than once it cast
  On my lowly cottage walls.

I pluck the fruit, the wine I waste,
  I drag through the weary hours ;
But the fruit is bitter to my taste,
  And I tire of the scent of flowers.

And I'd take my poverty instead
  And all that I have resign,
To feel as I felt when I coveted
  The wealth that now is mine.

.THE FORTUNE IN THE DAISY.

Of what are you dreaming, my pretty maid,
   With your feet in the summer clover?
Ah! you need not hang your modest head:
   I know 'tis about your lover.

I know by the blushes on your cheek,
   Though you strive to hide the token;
And I kuow because you will not speak,
   The thought that is unspoken.

You are counting the petals, one by one,
   Of your dainty, dewy posies,
To find from their number, when 'tis done,
   The secret it discloses.

You would see if he comes with gold and land —
   The lover that is to woo you;
Or only brings his heart and his hand,
   For your heart and your hand to sue you.

Beware, beware, what you say and do,
   Fair maid, with your feet in the clover;
For the poorest man that comes to woo,
   May be the richest lover!

Since not by outward show and sign
   Can you reckon worth's true measure,
Who only is rich in soul and mind,
   May offer the greatest treasure.

Ah! there never was power in gems alone
   To bind a brow from aching;

Nor strength enough in a jeweled zone
  To hold a heart from breaking.

Then be not caught by the sheen and glare
  Of worldly wealth and splendor ;
But speak him soft, and speak him fair,
  Whose heart is true and tender.

You may wear your virtues as a crown,
  As you walk through life serenely ;
And grace your simple rustic gown
  With a beauty more than queenly —

Though only one for you shall care,
  One only speak your praises ;
And you never wear, in your shining hair,
  A richer flower than daisies !

A PICTURE.

Her brown hair plainly put away
  Under her broad hat's rustic brim ;
That threw across her placid brow
  Its veil-like shadow, cool and dim :

Her shut lips sweet as if they moved
  Only to accents good and true ;
Her eyes down-dropt, yet bright and clear
  As violets shining out of dew :

And folded close together now
  The tender hands that seemed to prove
Their wondrous fitness to perform
  The works of charitable love.

Such is her picture, but too fair
  For pencil or for pen to paint ;
For who could show you all in one
  The child, the woman, and the saint?

I needs must fail ; for mortal hand
  Her full completeness may not trace,
Whose meek and quiet spirit gives
  Heaven's beauty to an earthly face !

FAITH.

DEAR, gentle Faith ! on the sheltered porch
  She used to sit by the hour,
As still and white as the whitest rose
  That graced the vines of her bower.
She watched the motes in the sun, the bees,
  And the glad birds come and go ;
The butterflies, and the children bright
  That chased them to and fro.
She saw them happy, one and all,
  And she said that God was good ;
Though she never had walked on the sweet green
    grass,
  And, alas ! she never would !

She saw the happy maid fulfill
  Her woman's destiny ;
The trusting bride on the lover's arm,
  And the babe on the mother's knee.
She folded meek, her empty hands,
  And she blest them, all and each,

While the treasure that she coveted
　Was put beyond her reach.

" Yea, if God wills it so," she said,
　" Even so 'tis mine to live.
What to withhold He knoweth best,
　As well as what to give ! "

At last, for her, the very sight
　Of the good, fair earth was done.
She could not reach the porch, nor see
　The grass, nor the motes in the sun
Yet still her smile of sweet content
　Made heavenly all the place,
As if they sat about her bed
　Who see the Father's face ;
For to his will she bent her head,
　As bends to the rain the rose.
" We know not what is best," she said ;
　" We only know He knows ! "

Poor, crippled Faith ! glad, happy Faith !
　Even in affliction blest ;
For she made the cross we thought so hard
　A sweet support and rest.
Wise, trusting Faith ! when she gave her hand
　To One we could not see,
She told us all she was happier
　Than we could ever be.
And we knew she thought how her feet, that ne'er
　On the good, green earth had trod,
Would walk at last on the lily-beds
　That bloom in the smile of God !

TO AN ELF ON A BUTTERCUP.

CUNNING little fairy,
    Where the breezes blow,
Rocking in a buttercup,
    Lightly to and fro ;
Little folks for nothing
    Look not so demure ;
You are planning mischief,
    I am very sure !

You will soon be dancing
    Down beside the spring ;
On the velvet meadow,
    In a fairy ring ;
Spoiling where the ewes feed
    All the tender grass ;
And making charmèd circles,
    Mortals dare not pass.

Darkening light where lovers
    Modest, sit apart,
You will kiss the maiden,
    With your wicked art ;
Make her think her wooer
    Wofully to blame ;
Through her frowns and blushes,
    Crying out, " For shame ! "

Ah ! my little fairy,
    With your mystic charms,
You have slipped the infant
    From its mother's arms ;

And have left a changeling
  In its place at night;
While you turned the mortal
  To a tricksy sprite.

Thus you mix folks up so,
  Wicked, willful elf;
Never one of us can know
  If he be himself:
And sitting here and telling
  Of the tricks you do;
I wonder whether I am I,
  Or whether I am you!

PROVIDENCE.

" AH ! what will become of the lily,
    When the summer-time is dead?
  Must she lay her spotless robes away,
    And hide in the dust her head? "

" My child, the hand that bows her head
    Can lift it up anew ;
  And weave another shining robe
    Of sunshine and of dew."

" But, father, what will the sparrows do?
    Though they chirp so blithe and bold,
  When the shelter of the leaves is gone
    They must perish with the cold."

· The sparrows are little things, my child,
   And the cold is hard to bear ;
Yet never one of these shall fall
   Without our Father's care."

" But how will the tender lambs be clothed ?
   For you know the shepherd said,
He must take their fleeces all away,
   For us to wear instead."

" They are warm enough to-day, my child,
   And so soon their fleeces grow,
They each will have another one
   Before they feel the snow."

" I know you will keep me, father ;
   That I shall be clothed and fed ;
But suppose that I were lost from home,
   Oh, suppose that you were dead ! "

" My child, there is One who seeks you,
   No matter where you roam ;
And you may not stray so far away,
   That He cannot bring you home."

" For you have a better Father,
   In a better home above ;
And the very hairs of your precious head
   Are numbered by His love ! "

LAST POEMS.

DREAMS AND REALITIES.

O ROSAMOND, thou fair and good,
And perfect flower of womanhood,
   Thou royal rose of June,
Why didst thou droop before thy time?
Why wither in thy first sweet prime?
   Why didst thou die so soon?

For looking backward through my tears
On thee, and on my wasted years,
   I cannot choose but say,
If thou hadst lived to be my guide,
Or thou hadst lived and I had died,
   'Twere better far to-day.

O child of light, O golden head —
Bright sunbeam for one moment shed
   Upon life's lonely way —
Why didst thou vanish from our sight?
Could they not spare my little light
   From heaven's unclouded day?

O friend so true, O friend so good —
Thou one dream of my maidenhood,
   That gave youth all its charms —
What had I done, or what hadst thou.
That through this lonesome world till now
   We walk with empty arms?

And yet, had this poor soul been fed
With all it loved and coveted —
   Had life been always fair —
Would these dear dreams that ne'er depart,
That thrill with bliss my inmost heart,
   Forever tremble there ?

If still they kept their earthly place,
The friends I held in my embrace,
   And gave to death, alas !
Could I have learned that clear, calm faith
That looks beyond the bounds of death,
   And almost longs to pass ?

Sometimes, I think, the things we see
Are shadows of the things to be ;
   That what we plan we build ;
That every hope that hath been crossed,
And every dream we thought was lost,
   In heaven shall be fulfilled ;

That even the children of the brain
Have not been born and died in vain,
   Though here unclothed and dumb ;
But on some brighter, better shore
They live, embodied evermore,
   And wait for us to come.

And when on that last day we rise,
Caught up between the earth and skies,
   Then shall we hear our Lord
Say, "Thou hast done with doubt and death ;
Henceforth, according to thy faith,
   Shall be thy faith's reward."

THE LAST ACT.

A WRETCHED farce is our life at best,
    A weariness under the sun ;
I am sick of the part I have to play,
    And I would that it were done.

I would that all the smiles and sighs
    Of its mimic scenes could end ;
That we could see the curtain fall
    On the last poor act, my friend !

Thin, faded hair, a beard of snow,
    A thoughtful, furrowed brow ;
And this is all the world can see
    When it looks upon you now.

And I, it almost makes me smile,
    'Tis counterfeit so true,
To see how Time hath got me up
    For the part I have to do.

'Tis strange that we can keep in mind,
    Through all this tedious play,
The way we needs must act and look,
    And the words that we should say.

And I marvel if the young and gay
    Believe us sad and old ;
If they think our pulses slow and calm,
    And our feelings dead and cold !
20

But I cannot hide myself from you,
    Be the semblance e'er so good ;
For under it all and through it all
    You would know the womanhood.

And you cannot make me doubt your truth,
    For all your strange disguise ;
For the soul is drawn through your tender voice,
    And the heart through the loving eyes.

And I see, where other eyes behold
    Thin, whitened locks fall down,
A god-like head, that proudly wears
    Its curls like a royal crown.

And I see the smile of the tender lip,
    'Neath its manly fringe of jet,
That won my heart, when I had a heart,
    And that holds and keeps it yet.

Ah ! how shall we act this wretched part
    Till its weary, weary close ?
For our souls are young, we are lovers yet,
    For all our shams and shows !

Let us go and lay our masks aside
    In that cool and green retreat,
That is softly curtained from the world
    By the daisies fair and sweet.

And far away from this weary life,
    In the light of Love's white throne,
We shall see, at last, as we are seen,
    And know as we are known !

www.ingramcontent.com/pod-product-compliance
Lightning Source LLC
Chambersburg PA
CBHW060547030726
47498CB00005B/1300